ALL THE LADIES LOVE COVENTRY

ALL THE LADIES LOVE COVENTRY

BLUESTOCKINGS DEFYING ROGUES 5

DAWN BROWER

MONARCHAL GLENN PRESS

For everyone who has waited for the Earl of Coventry's book. I hope this book is everything you hoped for, even if, it is on the shorter side. Coventry had his over version of a happily-ever-after. May all of you find yours too.

ACKNOWLEDGMENTS

Thanks to my cover artist extraordinaire: Victoria Miller. You have helped me along this long and I've learned a lot from you. Without you I fear how many mistakes I'd have made in my writing.

Also huge shout out to Elizabeth Evans who helps me with so many things. Thank you for sticking with me through so many writing projects. You're a gem I never expected to find.

CONTENTS

Prologue · 1
Chapter 1 · 9
Chapter 2 · 19
Chapter 3 · 29
Chapter 4 · 39
Chapter 5 · 50
Chapter 6 · 61
Chapter 7 · 73
Epilogue · 88

DAWN BROWER   *Excerpt: When an Earl Turns Wicked*

Prologue · 95
Chapter 1 · 110

EXCERPT: ODDS OF LOVE

Prologue · 125

EXCERPT: CHANCE OF LOVE

Prologue · 139

Afterword   151
About The Author   153
Also by Dawn Brower   155

"I cannot fix on the hour, or the spot, or the look or the words, which laid the foundation. It is too long ago. I was in the middle before I knew that I had begun."

— PRIDE AND PREJUDICE, JANE AUSTEN

PROLOGUE

April 1794

Charles Lindsay, the Earl of Coventry surveyed the building he was hoping to purchase. The structure was sound and would work splendidly for what he had in mind for it. The street it was located on was also ideal. A secret gentleman's club would be well hidden in the neighborhood, and its residents wouldn't question the constant comings and goings that would be involved. He had a lot of plans and this townhouse was only the beginning.

"The owner is willing to part with it?" He turned toward the solicitor in charge of the sale. Charles didn't want to seem too eager. It might give the solicitor a reason to raise the price. He wouldn't pay a penny more than it was worth.

"He is, my lord," he answered. His salt and pepper hair was sprinkled around his ears and the back of his head, but the top was completely bald. The solicitor had beady eyes that made him appear untrustworthy. Not a good look on someone that should invoke that particular feeling. "Would you like to make an offer?"

"No," he answered. "It needs major renovations and I'm not sure it'll work for what I have in mind." That was a lie, but he didn't want to make the man aware of his complete interest. "The entire bottom floor would need to be stripped and the walls rebuilt. Your employer is asking too much."

"I see..." The solicitor swallowed hard. Charles wished he could recall his name, but as it hadn't been important to him he'd dismissed it upon hearing it. He fumbled with some parchments and then glanced up. "Is there anything that will convince you to purchase it."

Charles held back a grin. It wouldn't work in his favor and he did want the property. He tapped his chin and tried to act as if he was considering his options. The truth was he knew exactly what his next move would be. That was the benefit of being several steps ahead of his opponent. He had a gift of seeing the larger picture and how all the pieces around him could fit together. This project of his was going to be big and he had to do everything right for it to work. "I might consider it if the owner will take off a thousand pounds from the selling price. I won't pay a shilling more than that."

He shuffled his feet and then met Charles gaze. "That sounds reasonable, my lord. I'll inform the owner that you're willing to purchase it."

Charles lifted a brow. "Is that all?" He shrugged and headed to the exit. As far as he was concerned their business had been concluded. If the owner took the offer the solicitor could send him a missive about it. He had a good feeling though. Soon he'd have the building necessary to start his club.

He hadn't reached the exit before the solicitor called out to him. "Lord Coventry."

He turned toward him and said, "Yes?"

"I have the authority to approve the sale within a certain amount. If you want the property it's yours."

This time he did allow the smile to form on his face. The Coventry Club was now one step closer to becoming a reality. He couldn't wait to tell his good friend the George, the Earl of Harrington about it.

They could plan the development and reconstruction of the townhouse together.

"Wonderful," he told the solicitor. "I'll let my solicitor know and you two can handle the details." Charles nodded at him. "Thank you for your assistance." With those words he did exit the building and headed home. He had an appointment later with George and they could make their final plans then.

***

Charles tapped his finger on his desk impatiently. Where the bloody hell was George? He was supposed to arrive several hours ago. He sighed and poured a glass of brandy from the decanter on his desk. They would have to discuss his plans for Coventry Club later. He sipped on his brandy and wondered what could have held his friend up. For the life of him he couldn't discern a reason for George to stay away. His friend never missed an appointment. He was the most reliable man of Charles acquaintance.

He set his glass down and peered at the deed to his new property. He'd already sent out missives to start the repairs and renovations. In a matter of months, no more than a year, his dream would be a reality. A safe haven for men who had no place else,

4

a den of iniquity for those that needed it, but mostly a place where loyalty would prevail more than anything else.

The door to his study flew open and George stepped inside. His face lit up with a huge grin as he exclaimed, "I'm a father Charles."

He'd forgotten George's wife was enceinte. That was a damn good reason for his friend to be late. Now that he realized why he felt like a right arse. Charles reached for a glass and poured two fingers of brandy into it, then handed it to his friend. He lifted his own glass and toasted, "To fatherhood." He sipped his brandy, and then asked. "I must ask—an heir or a daughter?"

"It's a boy," George answered. "The most perfect little bundle of joy I've ever held. We named him Jonas after my maternal great grandfather. It'll make my mum happy."

Charles knew he should look for a wife and carry on his line, but the idea of tying himself to one woman for the rest of his life didn't appeal to him. He hadn't met a woman that inspired that kind of commitment. George had married his wife because of his father's demands. The Duke of Southington was a difficult man to say no to. Charles didn't envy his friend's situation in that regard. "I'm sure she'll be ecstatic to just have a grandchild to dote on. I hear women like that sort of thing."

"You're probably correct in that assumption. Either way I'm grateful it's a boy. The birth was hard on Sarah. I don't think she could handle another pregnancy." He sighed. "Jonas is a blessing for us both. My father will finally leave us alone about carrying on the family line."

"Your father is brutal." He was an overbearing arse who browbeat George whenever he could. Charles wished he could find a way to remove the Duke of Southington from his friend's life. Unfortunately, it wasn't up to him to extricate George from the control of his father. His friend had to find the bollocks to do it himself. It was the only way he would ever know what it felt like to be free to make his own decisions.

"I have news," Charles began. "I've purchased the building I need for Coventry Club."

"You did?" His face lit up with happiness. "That's wonderful. Now you can achieve your goals and we'll all have a place to escape the realities of life."

"I'll have to discern the rules of the club before we invite new members. I'd like you to be the first head of the club if you're willing." He wanted

George to have the responsibility so he felt included, and it would give him something else to focus on other than the terror his father was.

"Me?" George asked surprised. "You don't want to run your own club?"

"I'd much rather enjoy it at first. One day I'll take over the duties, but I'd like the time to experience it first. You're much more level headed than I am and will be able to enforce whatever rules we put in place. I think the first one will be—the leader of the club is the only one that can be married. I don't want a bunch of cheating husbands to take their mistresses to the club."

"So once they marry they have to hand in their key?" George asked. "That's not a bad idea. So you're not going to take over until you find a bride? That's going to be a long ways off isn't it?"

Charles smiled. "I know one day I'll have to marry someone, but you're correct, I don't plan on finding a lady to wed for some years to come. I'm going to depend upon you to keep things running smoothly until then. But there isn't a requirement to wed to hold the position. If you find it is too difficult I can take over. If I marry before that...I'll have to take over is all."

"Yes," George agreed. "That makes sense." He

nodded at Charles. "All right I'll run your club." His lips tilted upward into another grin. "I can't wait to get started."

Charles picked up his glass and tipped it at his friend. "I already have my friend. Now let's drink to that new son of yours."

"That is a fabulous idea," George replied. He picked up his glass and clinked it with Charles's. "And to your future club. It'll be as successful as you imagined it would be."

They both drank the contents of their glasses, and then Charles filled them again with brandy. They drank several glasses before George left. They had all the rules of the club in place by then and the future of his Coventry Club would be a reality before long. Charles loved when a good plan came to fruition.

CHAPTER 1

April 1800

Lady Abigail Wallace stared down at her insipid white gown and frowned. The only color she'd been allowed to don was a sapphire sash that had been tied around her waist. It did little to make her gown more appealing. At least the color of the sash matched her eyes. White made her skin appear almost sickly though. She had fair skin and a sprinkle of freckles across her face. No one would mistake her for a fair English miss, especially with her brazen red hair.

Why had she let her father convince her to do a London season? There was nothing the ton had to offer she couldn't find at home—in Scotland. What was wrong with finding a good Scottish Laird as a husband? Her family's estate was in the lowlands and her father identified with their English brethren more than the Scottish highlanders, but Abigail would rather have taken a chance in Edinburgh.

"Quit fidgeting," her sister, Belinda, hissed under her breath. Her Scottish accent evident even in the low tone she spewed. "No, one will ask us tae dance with yer attitude."

She wanted to reply that would make her happy. None of the gentlemen appealed to her. All she wanted was to survive the season and go home. When she returned unmarried her father would have to agree to a season in Edinburgh. He wanted his eldest daughter married after all. Belinda he'd allow several seasons. She was the true beauty and would garner many suitors. Her sister had lovely blonde hair and fair blue eyes. She looked more like an English lady and nothing at all like Abigail. Where Belinda took after their English born mother, Abigail had received her auburn hair from her father. That wasn't all she'd received from him. Her temperament was a direct result of her Scottish blood. She'd never fit in with polite society. Abigail didn't suffer fools, and most of the dandies in attendance fit that description.

"Ye need not worry, sister dear," Abigail began, "There are plenty of gentlemen keeping their gazes on ye. It won't be long before one is brave enough tae ask for a set with ye." That was the truth too. Several gentlemen had been glancing in their direction, but their gazes always stayed a little longer on Belinda. Abigail had turned one and twenty before they'd departed for their London season. Belinda was three years younger than her. Both of them should already at least be betrothed, but when their mother died their father had been reluctant to see them go. Now he was determined they both find a husband, as was right, in his opinion. Abigail wanted to tell him where he could put his ideas about marriage, and it wasn't any place nice.

"Perhaps," her sister agreed. "If ye stop glaring at them they'll make the effort." Her sister glanced at her with a scowl resting on her gorgeous face. "Ye may not wish tae wed a gentleman of means, but I do. Dinna take this away from me."

A commotion stirred amongst the crowded ballroom. They all turned to stair at the entrance. Someone important must be arriving to make them all stop and stair with anticipation. Abigail wished she could say she didn't care, but her curiosity got the best of her. Who could be arriving that garnered so much attention. Many of the ladies started to whisper behind their fans and nearly squealed with excitement. Was the Prince Regent himself making an appearance? Nothing else made sense to her.

One of the Loxton servants opened the doors above the long sweeping staircase and announced, "The Earl and Countess of Harrington." A tall man with dark hair and a beautiful ethereal woman with silver blonde hair descended the stairs. Then a man followed behind them. That man caught her attention. He was beautiful—if a man could be described as such. Not classically beautiful, but in a way that took her breath away. He had high cheekbones and the most kissable lips she'd ever witnessed upon a male of good breeding. His dark hair was the color of a midnight sky and she found herself curious about the shade of his eyes. The man hadn't been announced, but he seemed to be the one everyone had been waiting for. They held their breath as he followed behind the earl and countess. Who was he?

"Oh he's lovely," her sister nearly breathed the words out. "Who do ye suppose he is?"

"I dinna have any idea," she said. Her words came out just as breathy as her sisters. "Perhaps we should find out."

"How?" Belinda lifted a brow. "We dinna have the connections tae ask and our chaperone won't be much help." She gestured toward the matron who'd accompanied them. She was snoring on a nearby settee oblivious to what her charges were doing. Not that Abigail and Belinda did much. No one had asked them to dance or really tried to talk to them. They were immediate wallflowers at the start of their come out in society. She hated to tell Belinda, but they may not leave with husbands. Belinda still had the best chance. Maybe Abigail should stay home next time and the dandies would be more comfortable approaching her sister.

"Let's dae little listening tae the ladies. They all seem tae love him," Abigail answered her. "They're fairly enraptured by his presence." She didn't blame them. The man really was lovely to behold, but they should have a little self-restraint. The man clearly ignored them all because he knew that he had their attention. It was then she realized he was as conceited as he was handsome. That would mean he'd expect a woman to dote on him. Abigail might find his visage appealing, but she refused to be any man's pawn. "He might make a fine suitor for ye."

"Dae ye think so?" Belinda asked as she tilted her

head. "He seems even more unlikely tae pay me any mind than the rest of the gentlemen."

Abigail didn't answer her sister. She was too busy trying to overhear the conversation between two of the ladies near them.

"Isn't he handsome," one of the ladies cooed.

"And dreamy," her companion said. "Don't forget that." She sighed as she stared at the man making his way through the ballroom.

Abigail rolled her eyes. They were ridiculous and way to obvious in their affections. She didn't want to think about how she'd been momentarily stunned by the man. That didn't matter because she had the good sense to snap out of it. Still she paid attention to their conversation because they still hadn't mentioned the man's name. She wanted it for Belinda. At least that was what she kept telling herself...

"No one ever knows when he'll come to a ball. He's one of the most eligible bachelors." The lady lifted her fan and waved it over her face. "Do you think if I present myself to Lady Harrington she'll introduce us? Everyone knows he doesn't come to any society functions unless it is with the earl and his wife."

The ladies were long winded, and while a font of

information, not the details she craved. She'd have to figure his name out another way. He'd made progress through the room and appeared to be leaving the ballroom as fast as he'd arrived. Was he not staying? He slid out the doors heading toward the garden. Did she dare meet him out there and have a clandestine meeting with him? It wouldn't work unless she could manage to act coy and uninterested in him. Many ladies before her would have already tried, and failed.

"Tonight hasn't been successful," her sister said breaking Abigail from her thoughts. Perhaps we should just go home."

"The ball has barely begun," Abigail replied. She had other ideas and she needed her sister otherwise occupied. "I think it's time ye found a dance partner." She looped her arm around Belinda's and pulled her over to the two ladies she'd been listening too. "Hello," she greeted them. "I'm Abigail and this is my sister Belinda." She hated introducing herself. She didn't like people in general and would much rather be at home—alone. But this was for her sister and well, herself, if she were to be honest. She wanted to talk to the mysterious man and gain a little more information on him. See for herself if he was worth dreaming over.

The two ladies had matching startled expressions on their faces. The dark haired beauty regained her composure first. "I'm Lady Matilda Emerson," she supplied. Drat. She'd forgotten to use their full titles when introducing them. Abigail was horrid at these things... "And this is my cousin, Lady Carolyn Westwick."

"It's lovely tae make yer acquaintance." Belinda smiled at them both. Her Scottish brogue came out as she spoke. At least she had a lovely voice... "We're new tae town." They probably already realized that much... Abigail held back a sigh and let her sister continue. "Would ye like tae pay a call on us? We're ever so naïve about everything and could use some sage advice."

All right... Maybe her sister knew exactly how to handle the situation. The ladies would probably think it was a good way to guide them through the web the ton weaved. There were so many things that should or should not be done it could be difficult to keep track of them.

Lady Matilda glanced at her cousin, then back at Abigail and Belinda. "It would be better if you called upon us." Then she gave them their address. One goal accomplished, so many more to see completed. In the end it would be all right. Belinda would find a husband and Abigail could return home. There was nothing in London for her.

The man that had caught her attention earlier came back into view. She nibbled on her lip and turned her head away. He wasn't for her.

"Oh..." Lady Carolyn sighed. "There he is again. He's so elusive—do you think he'll dance tonight?"

"It's not likely," Lady Matilda said. Her voice filled with admiration for the mysterious gentleman. "Lord Coventry doesn't dance. I wonder why he followed Lord and Lady Harrington tonight. He always has some reason for attending a ball though I've never been privy to the details when he has. My brother mentioned it before. Something about a club..."

The more she learned about this Lord Coventry —alas she finally had a name to attach to his person— the more intrigued she became. He was back in the ballroom so finding him alone probably wouldn't happen. Whatever chance she'd had vanished when he reappeared—that didn't mean she had given up. At some point she would have a conversation with him, and then, only then, would she be able to ascertain his worth. Abigail prided herself on being a good judge of a person's character.

Three gentlemen approached them and before

she had a chance to ask Lady Matilda or Lady Carolyn to expand on their earlier comments they were dragged off to the dance floor, followed by her sister. They left her alone near the edge of the floor. The one true wallflower in the bunch... Abigail sighed and decided leaving the ballroom was in her best interest. She didn't want anyone to pity her. Perhaps she'd go find the ladies' retiring room or the library. Maybe she could find a book to read until the end of the ball. Now that her sister had found a dancing partner she'd be occupied the rest of the evening. All those gentlemen who'd been secretly watching her wouldn't stay away now...

Resigned to spending the evening alone she left and didn't look back. Though she wanted to. Not to check on her sister, but to glance one last time at Lord Coventry, but she had some pride and she wouldn't give into the temptation he nearly burned with.

CHAPTER 2

Charles wished he didn't have to attend the bloody ball. He hated going out in society unless it was necessary. Unfortunately, it was important for him to attend. There was an earl in attendance he hoped to lure over to the club. So far he'd been unable to locate him, but that was to be expected. The Earl of Shelby was an even bigger rake than Charles could claim to be. Shelby's wife had died after giving birth to a daughter and he drowned his sorrows in brandy and women. He hadn't looked in on his son or daughter in over a year. George believed if they invited Shelby to join the club they could guide him on a different path. The club was more than a den of iniquity. It was also a place where a man had a soft place to fall if need be, and that didn't always mean the plushness of a woman's breasts, but they didn't hurt either.

Charles chuckled softly at that last thought. He wouldn't mind finding a warm and willing woman to share his bed with after he left the ball. He had to find Shelby and fast. He could almost feel all the stares from the ton ladies. No doubt they were all actively scheming to entrap him, at the very least into a dance. Charles didn't dance with any lady. It gave the rest of them ideas. He did charm them when necessary, and unfortunately, it often became that way at society events. He had to attend them from time to time so he did his best not to alienate any of them.

"Coventry," a male with a deep voice called out to him. He turned and met Lord Dashville's gaze. His dark hair was a little disheveled but he had a huge grin on his face. It had been a while since he'd seen his friend.

"Dash," he said and then smiled. "How are you? I hear you have a son."

"I do," he beamed. "We named him Oliver after my great grandfather. I was going to come by the club to see you, but, much to my surprise, I heard you'd be here. What brings you to the Loxton ball?"

Having Lord Dashville at the ball was a boon he

hadn't counted on. George would have to see to his wife for a good part of the event, but Dashville's wife would have remained at home so soon after the birth of their son "Have you seen the Earl of Shelby?"

"Actually, I have." He glanced over his shoulder to a set of doors. "He was heading to the library I presume for some assignation. He was foxed from what I could tell. He weaved a bit as he walked."

Coventry held back a sigh. They'd have a lot of work cut out for them if they accepted him into the club. Harrington better know what he was in for because they'd have to sober the earl up before they could even discuss the details of the club with him. Being wicked and an earl was a bonus normally, but Shelby would need to get his life straight before they agreed to allow him entrance. They didn't give a key out to the club lightly.

"I don't suppose you'd be willing to help me with him?"

"Is he going to be your new member?" Dashville couldn't be a part of the club because of his marital state. Somewhere along the way they'd only admitted earls to the club, but that hadn't been their original intention. Dashville was a marquess. If he hadn't been betrothed at the time the club opened he would have been invited to join. He wasn't turned away if he happened to show up at the club. It was more like he wasn't given full access and taken directly to Harrington's office. That was how any nonmember was treated and actually knew the club existed.

"We're considering him. Harrington believes he can be saved." Charles took a deep breath and then said, "I'm not so sure. I hope he can be because it would be a shame to lose a man with so much potential. Before his wife died he had so much promise. Now he is the worst reprobate in London."

"I thought you held that title." Dashville tapped Charles's shoulder with his hand and chuckled.

He glanced at his friend and grinned. "Somehow he's surpassed me. Though I do stop at seducing innocents. It wasn't difficult to take my claim to that particular title."

They left the ballroom and headed in the direction Dashville had noticed Shelby going. They turned a corner and didn't see him anywhere. The room was eerily quiet. There were not even any servants around and Charles had to admit that it would be a good area to have a clandestine meeting. "Isn't the library around here somewhere?" Dashville asked.

"I believe it is. I'll go check there and why don't

you go look in the garden. If you find him take him to my house and have my valet start sobering him up. I'll meet you back there either way in an hour." He could only do so much to save Shelby. If Dashville or he failed to locate him he'd try again another day, but he wouldn't keep trying if Shelby was going to be too difficult.

"All right," Dashville agreed. "Good luck." He turned and left Charles alone in the hallway heading toward the back gardens. He hoped he did find Shelby or at least Dashville did. The earl did need help.

Charles frowned and then started to walk toward the library. He kept a leisurely pace even though he should be in more of a hurry to find the earl. His heart just wasn't in it and he didn't know why. Usually he thrived on the thought of saving a potential member of his club. He'd been struck with a bit of ennui lately and he couldn't shake it. Something wasn't right in his life but he didn't know what. He couldn't dwell on it at the moment though. Charles had to at least attempt to locate Shelby. The hallway was still quiet and that didn't bode well for finding the earl.

He took a few more steps and stopped. A woman stood near the entrance of the library. Charles couldn't make out her features, but her silhouette was clearly a female, and a nicely curved one too. Maybe Shelby really did have an assignation in place and Charles would find him in the library. He really hated to interrupt a man's pleasure but there was no helping it. Charles continued toward the library and followed the woman inside. She hadn't noticed his presence and there didn't seem to be anyone else in the room. The moonlight streaming through the window illuminated her features, but not enough for him too get a good enough look at her. He wanted to see her and discover if she was as lovely as her shadowy figure suggested. One thing he did know—she wore white. That usually was a color reserved for debutants, otherwise known as innocents. What was a virgin doing meeting Shelby in secret? Did she believe the earl would marry her? Charles would have to disabuse her of that notion.

He stepped closer and said, "Are you lost?"

She jerked at his question. Maybe she hadn't been expecting someone after all. A woman planning on meeting a man wouldn't be startled by the sound of a male voice. "Who's there?" she asked.

She had a lovely Scottish accent that sent shivers down his spine. There were not too many women from Scotland attending London balls. He hadn't heard of any new arrivals either. Not that she couldn't have just come out in London. Charles didn't keep tabs on any of the debutants. He just usually heard about them whether he liked to or not. "You didn't answer my question," he teased. "Deflecting a question with one isn't very becoming, my dear."

He walked over to the hearth and skimmed his fingers across the top until he located the tinderbox. Then he leaned over to work on starting a fire. It was bloody cold in the room and he had a feeling they'd be there for a little while. It would also help to light the room a little bit and he could gain a better look at the chit.

"What are ye doing?" she asked.

"I think a fire will make things better don't you?" He didn't stop what he was doing to look at her. Charles wanted a fire and he'd see one lit. After he was done he'd give her all of his attention.

"Dae ye even know what yer doing?" She'd come to stand beside him and was now leaning down critiquing his technique.

Charles chuckled lightly. He kind of liked her. She wasn't trying to preen before him and catch his interest. That was rather refreshing. "I have lit a few fires in my day." In more ways than one... "Trust me, I can handle this."

"Something tells me yer not just referring tae setting a blaze alight in the hearth." She took a step back. "Ye didn't answer my earlier question. Who are ye?"

He stood to his feet after the fire was burning brightly and placed the tinderbox back in place. Charles turned to glance at her and chastise her for her rude behavior, but didn't manage to utter a word. The fire made her absolutely breathtaking. Her dark red hair was like a flame that crackled in the light and her fair skin was delectable. It was almost inviting him to taste it, but he held back. That was his own desires, not hers, springing forth. He swallowed hard and then cleared his throat. His cock tightened in his breeches and he prayed she didn't notice. "I trust from your continued deflection you're not lost."

"No," she agreed. "And I trust yer fancy way of changing the topic of our conversation is yer way of avoiding introducing yerself." A soft smile formed on her face and made her even lovelier. "But ye needn't worry. Yer name matters not tae me."

"Is that so?" He lifted a brow. "Why is that?"

She shrugged and turned away from him and

headed to the window. The young lady stared outside and up at the dark sky. "Because I'm not staying in London. There's nothing here for me. Once my sister finds a husband I'm returning home and never coming back."

That almost sounded like a challenge. "You are keeping your distance so you're not tempted to stay." It was something he would do. She was a kindred spirit and he respected it, even if he disagreed. A woman as vibrant as she was shouldn't close herself off from the world.

"That's one way of perceiving things." She continued to look out the window and apparently wanted to ignore him. That bothered Charles far more than he wanted to admit.

"A little conversation never hurt anyone," he began. "Becoming acquainted with me won't ensure you'll become enraptured with me or London. Why not take a gamble and discover something new."

"I'd rather not," she said. "I'm not the wagering sort. Risks are not something that lead anywhere good in my experience."

She was being too elusive and he wanted to crack her carefully crafted shell. If he wanted to start picking away at it he'd have to give her the tools to do so. "You may not wish to know me in truth," he began, "But I think we're going to be the best of friends." He bowed to her. "Let me introduce myself. I'm the Earl of Coventry, but you my dear, may call me Charles."

She glanced over her shoulder at him. Her lips parted, but no words came out. Then she smiled. "And I'm late returning tae the ball my lord. Dinna bother calling me anything. I doubt we'll meet again."

With those words she brushed past him and left him alone in the library. Charles had never been more intrigued in his life. He would discover her name and they would meet again. He'd do is damned best to ensure it.

CHAPTER 3

B right rays of sunshine streamed through the windows of the sitting room and illuminated the entire area. It was far too bright to read and Abigail had trouble holding in her irritation. How was she to learn anything about Greek mythology if she couldn't focus on the words? She grumbled and closed the tome with frustration, then tossed it on the empty chair next to her.

"Lovely," Belinda said. A satisfied smile filled her face. "Now that yer done trying tae be scholarly would ye like tae join me for a walk at Rotten Row?"

Abigail scrunched up her nose and then sighed. She might as well go with Belinda for some exercise. There wasn't a chance she could read anymore with the sun blinding her. Maybe she'd read more later in her room. She wouldn't be able to do much by candlelight. It would strain her eyes a bit, but she could get some more reading in for a short time. "All right," she agreed. "I'll join ye for a walk. Tell Bessie that we need her and a footman tae accompany us. We need tae make sure tae keep yer reputation intact so ye can secure one of these London gentleman as a husband."

Belinda lifted a brow. "Ye dinna care tae keep yer own reputation intact? Why ever not?"

Because she'd decided that she didn't care if she ever married. The man from the other night—the Earl of Coventry—had intrigued her, but he was clearly a rogue. All the London ladies might want a chance at taming him, but Abigail had better things to do with her time. She'd gained his attention and that was enough for her. It was all too easy to get him to notice her and she hadn't really been trying. "I have my reasons." It was the only answer she intended to give her sister.

"Ye may think ye keep yer emotions inside," her sister began. Her lips tilted upward into a smug smile. "But I know ye. I saw how ye looked at that gentleman the other night at the Loxton ball. He appealed tae ye. Maybe we can still discover his identity and discern a way for ye tae gain his attention."

Of course her sister had noticed her interest in Lord Coventry. The earl was handsome as sin, and he probably did sin better than most men, but there was more to a man than his pleasing appearance. "I dinna need help with that. I dinna want tae gain his attention."

Her sister tilted her head to the side and studied her. "Ye are hiding something. What dae ye know?"

"Not a thing," she reassured Belinda. "Are we going tae Rotten Row or not?"

"All right," Belinda acquiesced. "I'll allow ye tae keep yer secrets—for the moment." She stood and then met Abigail's gaze. "But I will uncover the truth and then I'll want answers."

Abigail shrugged. "There's nothing tae find." There really wasn't. Even if Belinda discovered she'd had an encounter with Lord Coventry in the library there wasn't anything that would come of it. No one saw them—thank God. The last thing she needed was a forced marriage. They'd both end up miserable in the end. Abigail fully intended to live a long and happy life and that did not include a marriage of convenience. Though only bright side to a union with Lord Coventry was her attraction to him. The rest would be completely superficial.

Belinda shook her head and headed out of the sitting room. "Meet me in the foyer. I'll go find our chaperones for our walk."

Abigail shook her head lightly. Her younger sister thought she knew everything, but she didn't. There were some things far more important than having a fine husband. Abigail wanted something more meaningful in her life. She loved books and learning new things. If she married her husband might not like her doing those things. Once a woman became a man's wife she would be forever under his rule. She became the man's property. Something about that always bothered Abigail. Other women liked to belong to someone, to be taken care of, and never having to worry about anything. That wasn't so easy for Abigail to do. It would be nice to be loved and appreciated, but a society marriage didn't always include those things. Love was a rare emotion in marriage.

She'd dwelled on everything far too much. Abigail retrieved her book and carried it to her room. Once there she placed the book on her writing desk, then went to her armoire to find her pelisse. It might be a little chilly out and she didn't want to be cold on her walk. After she found it she went back down stairs and found her sister waiting for her in the foyer. Bessie and one of the footman were also with her.

"Finally," Belinda said with exasperation in her voice. "We can depart. Whatever took ye so long?"

"I didn't realize I'd dawdled." She held back the urge to roll her eyes. Belinda could be so dramatic at times. "Please lead the way dear sister.

Belinda opened the door and exited. Abigail, Bessie, and the footman followed behind her. The pace her sister had set was far faster than Abigail had expected. She had to wonder if her sister had another reason for wanting to go to Rotten Row. Had she perhaps met a man she hoped would court her? When they arrived she'd be able to ascertain the answer. Maybe it would be her, not Belinda that uncovered something titillating. Her sister hoped to discover something of a secret about her. Well, maybe her dear sibling had something of her own to hide and was deflecting. She smiled to herself. Now that she had a mystery to solve she was rather looking forward to their little jaunt in Rotten Row. She usually loathed their outing there. This time there would be something far more intriguing to keep her attention. It almost made up for her interrupted study time...almost.

***

Charles sat astride his horse and kept it at a light walk as he steered him down the path at Rotten Row. George was beside him on his own horse. They had decided to get some exercise and attempt to breathe something resembling fresh air or what London offered as such. Dashville had been able to locate the Earl of Shelby and had delivered him to Coventry Manor. They'd sobered him up and put him to bed. He'd been sleeping ever since. They had yet to have a conversation with him about his future as one of the wickedest of earls England had to offer, and well, joining the exclusive club that Coventry had helped to create and maintain.

"How is he doing?" George asked. His lips tightened into a thin white line. "Do you think he'll be able to have a lucid conversation about joining the club later today?"

Neither one of them were particularly happy about the state of Shelby's state of mind. They might already be too late to save him, but George believed it was never really too late. Charles wasn't always so optimistic. There were some things a man could never return from. Losing a wife, one that was adored, was one of them. Shelby wasn't the same man they'd attended school with. They're Eton days were so far away they almost seemed like they happened to someone else entirely. "He should be all right by tonight. I'll make sure he's ready to have a serious discussion. Make sure you come over before nightfall and we'll have a conversation with him about his future. I hope he's receptive."

"As do I," George said and then sighed. "It's so sad what's happened to him."

Charles hoped he never found himself in a similar state. He never wanted to fall in love. He adored women, but he'd never loved any of them. Charm went along way to gain him the things he desired most. He didn't need love to have a fulfilling life. From the way Shelby was destroying his life he suspected it was the one thing capable of doing the exact opposite. No, love was not something he wanted to find. "His situation is wretched," Charles agreed. "But lucky for Shelby he has a good friend like you."

"And you," George supplied. "We'll make sure he finds his way back to living a more sustainable life. At the very least he has to make sure his two children are cared for. Gregory and Samantha need him."

"I can't imagine being responsible for a child." He wasn't sure he ever wanted to be a father. Charles would probably marry at some point. He'd need an heir to carry on the title after he was gone. A part of him thought it would be better to let the title go to his cousin. Children were an even bigger responsibility than a wife. They would expect far more from him, perhaps more than he was capable of giving.

"I love my son," George replied quietly. "Jonas is a blessing I never could have imagined having, but there is a duty to him that I had to commit to. You'll be all right with it one day."

"Perhaps," he said noncommittally. He stared toward the path where members of the ton were walking. The gleam of bright red hair caught his attention and he narrowed his gaze. It might be the lady from the previous night, the one who'd failed to introduce herself. "George do you know those two ladies coming toward us on the walking path?"

George looked at where he'd directed him and shook his head. "I did notice them at the Loxton ball, but I'm not acquainted with them. Sarah may be. Do you wish me to inquire? Has one caught your fancy?"

In a way, the red-haired lady had. It was more

she intrigued him. Why had she run away so fast? Had she been there to meet someone else and he'd interrupted her assignation? Something about her having a clandestine meeting with another man rankled him. He didn't like the idea of her in someone else's arms. "No," he answered. "She seemed familiar is all."

He doubted George would believe his excuse, but he didn't want to admit the truth. Any other lady of the ton would have been throwing themselves at him. It was refreshing to find one that didn't want anything to do with him. That could be part of her scheme too. Maybe she was acting disinterested to gain his interest. It worked if that was her intention. Charles fully intended to discover everything about her that he could. But first he would need her name.

"There is an easy way for us to answer your question," George supplied.

"How so?" He turned to meet his friend's gaze.

"We dismount and go over to talk to Lady Marvelle," he answered. "She's with them now."

Charles swung his gaze around to where he last saw the mysterious lady. Sure enough, her and the blonde lady she was walking with were in a rapt conversation with Lady Marvelle. It would be an easy enough answer to the dilemma of her unknown name. Lady Marvelle was a way to gain a proper introduction since she was his godmother. George was a genius. "All right," he agreed. "Let's dismount."

George chuckled and slid off his horse, and Charles did the same. They grabbed the horse's reins and led them over to where the ladies were talking. Soon he'd have a name to go with the face. After that he'd find out everything he could about her. Mostly, he wanted to discover what it was she was scheming inside her pretty head. Charles refused to be a dupe and no lady would ever make a fool of him. If this one thought he'd marry her she'd soon discover the error of her thinking. Charles had no intention of marrying anyone, at least not yet. He needed several years of bachelorhood before he subjected himself to one woman for the remainder of his days. For now though, he'd settle with some flirtation with a gorgeous, intelligent woman. Because he had no doubts about either one of those things in regards to the red-haired lady...

CHAPTER 4

Lord Coventry was heading in their direction. Abigail did her best to ignore his approach but she was aware of each step he took. Her heart beat heavily inside her chest and her cheeks heated. She was far more attracted to the earl than she liked or cared to admit. They had been in town for weeks and she'd not seen him once, but now she'd crossed paths with him twice in a matter of less than a day. Was fate trying to tell her something? She shook that thought away. No, there was no higher being or mythological entity steering her down a specific path. That was ridiculous and she wouldn't entertain that thought any longer. Abigail believed in facts and things that were provable. Fate was not something that could be studied and verified.

"Isn't that the gentleman that caught yer attention last night at the Loxton ball?" Her sister asked and nudged her with her shoulder. "I think he's coming this way. Dae ye suppose he wants tae converse with us?"

Lady Marvelle glanced at the gentleman approaching and then smiled. "Ah, it's Lord Harrington and Lord Coventry. Coventry is my godson. He probably wishes to say hello." She turned her attention back to Abigail and Belinda. "Did you mention one of them caught your eye? Harrington, of course, is already wed so he's not eligible, but Coventry needs a wife. I'll introduce you."

Wonderful. Abigail couldn't admit that she'd already met Lord Coventry because their introduction hadn't been proper. It would likely give Lady Marvelle the vapors to learn she'd been alone with the earl. "That would be lovely." There was not much else she could say to her other than that. It would be perfectly rude to tell her she had no desire to be introduced to her godson. Besides it would be a lie anyway. She did want a proper introduction. That way if they did cross paths with him again she could converse with him. She realized she was being contrary in her thoughts but Abigail always did her best not to lie to herself. She may not want to marry;

however, the earl did intrigue her. The very least she could do was discover what it was about him, other than his handsome visage, that she found so interesting.

The gentleman approached and bowed. "Lady Marvelle," Lord Harrington greeted her. "Coventry and I noticed you strolling with these two young ladies and felt it necessary to pay our respects."

"As you should," Lady Marvelle said and then beamed at them both. Her smile grew in large degrees she was pleased that they'd singled her out. Abigail wondered how many times in the past they'd ignored the elderly lady. "How was your ride this afternoon?"

"Pleasant and uneventful," Coventry replied smoothly. "We'll head back to Mayfair soon." The earl slid his gaze to Belinda, and then Abigail. His lips twitched slightly as he boldly stared into her eyes. "And who are your two companions." He didn't look back at Belinda at all. His focus was completely on Abigail. "I don't believe we've met."

"If you attended more society functions you would meet many eligible ladies," Lady Marvelle chastised him. "I did hear you were at the Loxton ball last night. What made you decide to attend?"

It was Abigail's turn to have her lips twitch

slightly. His eyes darkened at Lady Marvelle's words and he didn't seem too thrilled that she hadn't introduced them. She had to wonder what the older lady was planning. Before the two lords approached she said she'd introduce them, and that had been the perfect opportunity to do so.

"Nothing like you assume," Coventry replied. He scrunched his eyebrows together and shook his head slightly. "I accompanied Harrington and his countess. I was feeling a bit ennui. Don't concern yourself about it my lady. It won't likely happen again as I have no desire to seek a young miss as my intended."

Lady Marvelle sighed loudly. "A rogue never does seek out love my dear. It finds you when you least expect it to." She smiled almost haughtily. "But that's a discussion for another day. You wished to meet my companions." She turned to them and said, "This is Lady Belinda Wallace and Lady Abigail Wallace. This is their first season so they're perfectly safe from you as you said you're not looking for any young misses to make your countess."

Abigail lifted her hand to her mouth to stifle laughter from spilling out of it. Lady Marvelle put her godson in his place. He had no reason to inquire about her or her sister's identities when he didn't wish to court either of them. It was only polite to be introduced, but other than that they had nothing to offer each other. Lord Coventry didn't appreciate being reminded of his earlier words.

Instead of taking Lady Marvelle's chastisement gracefully he chose to ignore it. "There are other reason's to have a conversation with a lady other than courting, my dearest godmother."

"Oh?" She lifted a brow. "I suppose you're right but I can't recall any. A young unmarried lady should only spend time alone with a gentleman if he is courting her unless that male is her father, brother, grandfather...I trust ye follow my meaning." She lifted her chin. "Coventry the way you keep looking at Lady Abigail is akin to a wolf about to devour a sheep. If you don't have good intentions regarding her stay far away."

Abigail jerked her gaze toward Lady Marvelle. She hadn't realized how astute the elder lady was. Abigail had felt as if Lord Coventry's gaze was rather intense, but thought maybe she was reading it wrong. Surely he wouldn't be overly forward with her in polite company. She smiled lightly at Lady Marvelle and then said, "My lady ye needn't worry about Lord

Coventry leading me astray. He doesn't have anything tae offer me tae make me forget myself." She turned to meet his gaze and boldly stated, "If he had any sway over my emotions he'd have succeeded last night at the Loxton ball. No man can or will make me forget who I am or what I desire from life."

"That's not reassuring," Lady Marvelle answered. "However, you're also not my charges. I'll speak with your chaperone about her lax in duties. I'm afraid I must leave. I'm expected for tea at the Duchess of Montford's in an hour." She turned to Harrington. "Give a hug to that darling boy of yours for me and keep my godson out of trouble. His charm might lead him somewhere he will regret one day." With those words Lady Marvelle strolled away leaving Abigail and Belinda alone with the two earls.

With Lady Marvelle a safe distance away Coventry turned his attention back to Abigail. "No influence at all?" He lifted a brow.

"Not at all." Her gaze didn't waver once. "But dinna let that concern ye my lord. There are plenty of ladies that would appreciate yer attention. The entire ballroom was awed by yer grand appearance at the ball. It was quite titillating."

Harrington groaned at her words. "She's quite

right. You're all they discussed last night. Of course they stopped when Sarah and I approached, but we still overheard it all. You really should attend more functions and they won't become so excited when you do appear."

Belinda giggled and then shrugged lightly. "I'm grateful he did appear. My night was dreadful until then."

Harrington turned to her and asked, "How did his arrival help your evening?" He had a perplexed expression on his face.

"Abigail and I are the newest edition of wallflowers. No one ever asks us tae dance." She glanced at Abigail and frowned. "I think she scares them away with the scowl she always has on her face."

Coventry took that as his cue to once again join their conversation. "But it's a lovely scowl. It should intrigue them and not frighten them off. A true gentleman would enjoy the challenge."

"A true rogue ye mean," Abigail retorted. Coventry was a charmer and if she didn't remain careful he'd coax her down a path she might come to regret. "A gentleman would respect a lady's wish tae be left alone."

"Can't a man be a gentleman and a rogue?" Coventry asked. His lips tilted upward into a sinful smile. It sent shivers down her spine and her heart fluttered, skipping several beats as she tried to regain control of her traitorous body.

Abigail squared her shoulders and did her best to remain firm. "Not at the same time. A rogue has the potential tae be a gentleman, but once he gives in tae his baser instincts that façade slips away and the truth is revealed. It's either one or the other and never at the same time."

"For an innocent miss you sure do seem sure of this." He stepped a little closer and she had to resist the urge to take a step back in return. "How many clandestine meetings have you had in your short time out in society?"

"None," she answered automatically. "No gentleman are interested in me and even if they were I wouldn't allow myself tae be lured away."

For several moments it seemed as if it was just her and Coventry. Her sister and Harrington disappeared and she had to remind herself to breathe. The intensity between them was overwhelming and she didn't know what to do with it. She needed distance, lots and lots of distance.

What was it about this man that made her want to do things she knew was a bad idea. Abigail needed time and more information before she could discern the answer to that question. Coventry might not give it to her and if she really wanted that space to uncover what the unwanted emotions meant she'd have to demand it.

"Do you wish to wager on it?" Coventry lifted a brow.

"Wager?" She scrunched her eyebrows together. What was he speaking about now? "I'm afraid I dinna understand."

"On your ability to be lured into sin of course." His voice was a low rumble that vibrated over her skin. Abigail didn't think anyone else had heard him. Somehow he'd stepped closer to her without her noticing. "I'm willing to bet that I can entice you to experience desire—with me."

She turned toward him. There was less than a foot separating them now. Abigail swallowed hard and then answered, "I dinna need tae wager anything tae discern the answer."

"No?" He frowned and then stepped back. "That is too bad. It would have been amusing to become more acquainted."

"I'm not one of yer doxies my lord. I'm not a toy placed on yer path solely for yer pleasure." She glanced at her sister but she seemed to be engrossed in a conversation with Harrington and didn't pay any attention to the discussion she was having with Coventry. Appearances could be deceiving though. She suspected Belinda would want to discuss this development when they returned home.

He glowered at her with displeasure. "I never would have equated you with a whore Lady Abigail. I'm offended you did."

She shrugged. "I find I dinna particularly care if ye are offended." Abigail had to escape his scrutiny. She'd purposely changed the topic of their conversation so that he'd stop trying to charm her. If she allowed herself she'd willingly follow him down a path of wickedness. He tempted her far more than she wanted to admit. "It is I who should be offended by yer disregard for my status as a lady of good standing. Perhaps ye should consider that before ye approach another lady in society with yer offer of a wager."

He smiled at that. Abigail wanted to smack it off his face. What had she said to garner that reaction? "I think I'm starting to understand you. It wasn't that I offered the wager, it was that you wanted to take it."

Damn him. "Ye be wrong of course. If ye will excuse me I'm going tae retrieve my sister from yer friend's attention. If he keeps company with ye he is probably equally as bad." With those words she stomped away but his chuckles echoed behind her, infuriating her with each step she took.

CHAPTER 5

The ride in Hyde Park had been invigorating, but it was Charles's conversation with Lady Abigail that had left him exhilarated. He'd never expected to be so intrigued by a young lady. This particular one held his attention long after they parted ways. Charles couldn't wait to cross paths with her again. In fact, perhaps he should find a way to ascertain her schedule and manufacture a meeting with her. Yes, he liked that idea. He smiled at the thought of sharing barbs with her again. Lady Abigail had a sharp tongue. It was a good thing he had a tough hide or she'd have left him bloody from her dressing down. He'd send one of his servants around for more information on her schedule and hire a Bow Street runner to look into the lady's particulars.

He strolled into his study, George fast on his heels, and sat down behind his desk. Not long after that Shelby stumbled in and dropped on the settee on the far side of the room. He groaned and covered his eyes with his arm. "Why is it so bloody bright in here."

Charles lifted a brow and turned to glance at George. His friend shook his head indicating that he'd handle it. Well that was all right with him because Charles would have smacked Shelby in the head. The man wouldn't have appreciated it either. He had to be feeling rather wretched after his night of over indulgence.

"How are you feeling Lord Shelby?" George asked him. He kept his voice calm and soothing. Charles had witnessed him using that tone on a spooked horse once. It seemed fitting that he did so with Shelby as well. Shelby did appear a bit skittish.

"I'm all right," Shelby replied wariness etched through his voice. "Why am I here again?" He scrubbed his hands over his face and groaned. He held the palm of his hand to the top of his head. "All right, I lied, I feel bloody awful. My head is exploding."

Coventry held back a smile. It wouldn't further their cause and George was insistent that Shelby could be helped. He'd allow his friend to at least try. He'd done a lot for many individuals since they opened their club's doors. Shelby might end up being a wonderful addition. "We wanted to discuss your future with you." Charles tapped his fingers on his desk almost impatiently. He was having difficulty keeping himself relaxed. Dealing with Shelby wasn't what he wanted to do. No, he'd much rather seek Lady Abigail out and spar with her instead. "Now that you're coherent enough to have a conversation we shall proceed." He nodded at George. "Why don't you start."

"Lord Shelby," he began. "First I want to tell you that we're incredibly sorry about your loss."

"Are you?" Shelby replied bitterly. "Not as sorry as I am."

George chose to ignore that and instead continued with his well-practiced speech. He cleared his throat and said, "We have a club that we believe you'll fit in. You didn't meet some of the requirements before, but considering your widower status we thought you would benefit from our association."

Shelby lifted a brow. "You want me to join a

club? Like we're boys at Eton looking for something to hide in."

Charles chuckled. He had to admit that if he were in Shelby's place he'd be equally sardonic. "Not quite like that," he said. "More a den of iniquity with a loyalty thrown in. You, my friend, are in need of some camaraderie and the side benefits of what our particular club has to offer." He lifted a brow. "Be honest with yourself. What do you have to lose? If you keep at the pace you're on you'll be in a grave by the end of the year. It may have failed to cross your mind, but you have two small children who need you. At least do your best to go through the motions of life, and maybe over time it'll seem almost normal to you."

Shelby groaned and pushed his head into his open palms. George glanced at Charles and shook his head. They had to allow Shelby to come to his own conclusions. Once he decided to join the club, and he would join, they'd tell him the rules and bestow a key on him. George would also offer one of the upstairs bedrooms for him to let. They were usually reserved for confirmed bachelors who needed someplace to live, but they both believed Shelby might need to stay at the club more often than not over the next several months. He needed real interactions to help him settle into his life without his beloved wife.

"All right," Shelby finally said. His voice was hoarse and shook with emotion. It was also probably a bit raw from all the brandy he'd imbibed. "You're both correct. I've been a right arse since my wife died. I'm faltering and I don't know how to live without her."

Charles pictured Lady Abigail at his words. It stunned him a little that she would come to mind in this situation. What was it about her that he couldn't stop thinking of her? He didn't equate his situation with Shelby's, not entirely. Charles was fast becoming preoccupied with Lady Abigail, but he didn't love her. He didn't know what love entailed and he never wanted to. If he fell in love and lost that person... He shook the thought away. No, he would ensure he didn't experience what Shelby now was. "All you can do is get up each morning and go through the motions. One day you'll wake up and realized you only thought about her five times, then three, then none." He hated that Shelby was in so much pain. "It'll be the day you forget about her entirely that will be the worst. You'll hate yourself for it, but that's the way of life. We don't ever really forget those we've lost. It's more we find a way to hide the pain so we can continue without them. When that day comes you'll be even more grateful to have a group of individuals you can rely on."

Shelby took a deep breath and nodded. "I want to become a member of your club." His face had lost all color and his deep blue eyes watered a little, as he seemed to fight tears.

George smiled and then said, "Wonderful. Now that it is decided let me go over the rules with you." At least someone seemed happy with the outcome. Not that Charles was displeased, but he didn't have his friend's enthusiasm either.

While George informed Shelby of all the details, Charles decided to take care of his inquiries into Lady Abigail. Now that he decided to pursue her in a sense, he wasn't going to wait. He reassured himself that he wasn't courting her; no this was something entirely different. Charles just wanted to spend time in her company. To learn what she liked and enjoy a bit of titillating conversation... and maybe, just maybe, if he kept telling himself that he'd start to believe it. Charles feared that crossing paths with Lady Abigail was fate's way of thumbing its nose at him. The man who refused to be enthralled by a woman was quickly becoming a fool for an innocent hellion.

⁕

Abigail couldn't believe the gall of Lord Coventry. What he had said to her... It was rude and suggestive, and she'd liked it. How perverse was she to have enjoyed that rogue's words? What was wrong with her? She actually hoped they would meet each other again. She'd never felt so stimulated in both body and mind before. He had this affect on her... She couldn't explain it if she tried, and if she were to be honest with herself; she didn't want to define it. Abigail only knew one thing with a certainty: Lord Coventry made her want things she swore she didn't.

"Why are ye being so quiet?" Belinda asked. "Ye have been inside yer head since we left Hyde Park earlier."

She scrunched her nose up and turned her head to meet her sister's gaze. They'd been lounging in the sitting room awaiting their afternoon tea. Abigail had retrieved her book on Greek mythology, but hadn't opened it. She'd been too engrossed in her thoughts about Lord Coventry to try. He was even interrupting her scholarly pursuits. "I'm considering how to approach my studies." A blatant lie and Belinda would not take it as an appropriate answer to Abigail's silence.

"I doubt the veracity of yer claim, sister dear,"

Belinda replied in a singsong tone. "Ye are thinking of the Earl of Coventry. Ye can't fool me." She leaned forward and placed her elbow on the arm of her chair, then rested her chin on the palm of her hand. She winked and then said, "I dae believe ye have a beau."

"I dinna have one," she replied vehemently. Lord Coventry may have appeared to single her out, but he hadn't. A rogue didn't pay singular attention to a maiden or he'd be taken seriously in his attentions. All the ladies in town knew he wasn't truly looking for a female to court. They all batted their eyelashes and flirted, but they didn't expect anything from it. The earl was too much of a scoundrel to settle down, and too much of a gentleman not to make his intentions known. He skated a fine line between both. She'd been intrigued by him at the Loxton ball, and once she ascertained his identity it had been easy enough to gain some information about him. Both the males and females alike revered him, but they'd all been clear—Lord Coventry was not the marrying kind.

"I dae believe ye doth protest tae much," Belinda answered. "I'm right and ye are well aware of it. He'll come calling and then I will have ye eating crow."

Abigail feared her sister was correct in her

assessment of the situation. She wasn't ready to admit to anything aloud though. When or if anything of note happened between her and Lord Coventry she'd consider it then. This was all too new to make any lasting decisions yet. Nothing may come of it and she didn't want to hope anything would either. "Think what ye will," she told her sister. "I can't control that, but trust me on one thing, Lord Coventry is not going to be calling on me here." No, he'd be much sneakier in his version of a courtship. She could use other words to describe what he was doing, but she recognized it for what it was—even if he didn't quite yet.

Her sister had a self-satisfied smile on her face. She was being way too smug for Abigail's liking. "And ye thought ye would be able to return home. Father will be pleased."

"There's nothing for him tae consider. Dinna say a word tae him." She didn't want her father to have any expectations where Lord Coventry was concerned. He did have hopes that both Abigail and Belinda would marry well. She'd not have him anticipate a wedding and then not have one occur. "Lord Coventry is not courting me."

"I'll not mention it tae father the next time I write—yet." Belinda lifted both of her eyebrows a couple of times in a suggestive manner. Abigail held in a groan. She didn't want to encourage her sister. "But once he starts courting ye for all the ton tae see I'll not be able tae contain the news."

No, she wouldn't. If Lord Coventry really did court her, and Abigail still wasn't sure how she felt about the prospect of it, anyone who was acquainted with her would inform her father with glee. It might even be enough to bring him to London. "If that should occur I'll deal with it then. For now there is no news tae report."

A maid came into the room pushing the teacart. There were several different cakes on the tray along with the tea service. Abigail's stomach growled on cue. She was hungry and wanted to devour all of the little cakes. It would also silence her sister for a spell while she filled her mouth with the delectable treats. Maybe she should finish her tea and rush from the room before Belinda regained her equilibrium. She didn't want to discuss Lord Coventry any further. Truthfully, she wanted more time alone to be introspective of her own emotions. She could take her book on Greek mythology to her room and pretend to study. There was no way she'd actually be able to absorb anything intelligent in her brain as preoccupied as she was with Lord Coventry. Yes, that was a good plan.

"Are ye going tae eat any of the cakes?" Belinda eyed the tiny treats voraciously.

Abigail retrieved her teacup and took a slow sip ignoring her sister's question. Perhaps that was somewhat evil of her, but Belinda had been way too gleeful about Lord Coventry. This small retribution would help alleviate that sting. After several sips she answered her, "I'm not hungry. Eat as many as ye want." She set her teacup down and then stood. "I'm going tae retire tae my chambers with my book. I'll see ye at the evening meal." Then she slowly strolled out of the room as if she didn't have a care in the world. She really wanted to rush up to her room so she'd be in solitude, but she refused to let her sister know she was rattled in any way. Damn Lord Coventry for destroying her carefully laid plans. Whatever was she going to do with that man?

CHAPTER 6

I t had taken him less than a sennight to gather information regarding Lady Abigail. Her accent had told him she derived from Scotland, but not much else. Her father was the Earl of Hayfield, a Scottish lowlander with strong English ties. Other than her family connections, Charles had been unable to garner many details about her. A shrewd housemaid had been able to obtain Lady Abigail's schedule for the next fortnight though, and he fully intended to utilize it. He'd made sure to reward her underhandedness for two reasons: to keep her loyal and also quiet.

He glanced down at the stolen details and frowned. Why was he going through so much trouble? What was it about Lady Abigail that made him act in ways he'd never done prior to meeting her? If George were aware of his scheming he'd call him a besotted fool. How could he be though? He had only a few brief encounters with Lady Abigail. Once in the Loxton library, once in Hyde Park, and finally he'd crossed her path the other night at the theater. He hadn't known she'd be in any of those places, but now, he could arrange to be wherever she went. At least the social events... He had invitations to all of them. The matron's of the ton sent him an invite to everything hoping to lure him to their events. He almost never went, and even when he did, he had a specific purpose for attending. Once he achieved his goal he promptly left and didn't bother with much socializing while there. He didn't understand why any of them bothered inviting him to their events, but he also didn't discourage it either.

Her next event was a garden party at the Duchess of Breckenridge's home on the outskirts of London. It had been a while since he'd ventured out of the city. It might be good to breathe something resembling fresh air. He was curious enough about Lady Abigail to attend a bloody garden party. Charles never would have believed it of himself if he weren't already in the midst of it.

"What has you scowling?"

Charles glanced up from the list and met George's gaze. He pushed it under his stack of invitations and answered him, "Nothing much. Debating attending a social event."

"Oh?" George lifted a brow. "Is there a prospective recruit for the club?"

The question was a reasonable one. There hadn't been any other reason for Charles to attend a social event. The problem was he didn't quite know how to answer his friend. "No," he replied, and then frowned. "I am feeling a little restless and thought it might help to attend something other than a club soiree."

"I see..." His friend cleared his throat and that said more than his words did. Charles hadn't given him an answer he believed, and he honestly didn't blame George for doubting him.

"How is Shelby?" he attempted to change their topic of conversation. The Earl of Shelby was a save subject for them to discuss. "Has he settled into his room at the club?"

"He's doing much better." George walked the rest of the way into the room and sat in a nearby chair. "His drinking has abated and he's sober more often than not these days. I think he'll be all right."

Charles had his doubts, but he was glad that Shelby had stopped with his excessive drinking of brandy. He would have hated to see Shelby throw his life away. "Wonderful. Hopefully he doesn't fall back into bad habits."

"I don't believe he will." George gestured toward his desk. "What were you looking at when I came in?"

He'd hoped George hadn't been paying that close attention to what he'd been doing when he arrived. He should have known better. George was perceptive. "Just my list of invitations." He shrugged. "I have a huge stack of them to go through as usual."

"What one were you considering attending?" He motioned to the stack again. "Let me see."

Luckily the garden party invitation was at the top of the stack. Charles retrieved it and held it out for George. He plucked it from his fingertips and held it out to read. "The Duchess of Breckenridge's event?" He tilted his head to the side. "There is bound to be a lot of eager young debutantes there. Are you sure you wish to go to it? They'll flock to your sides like ducks after pieces of bread."

That was the conundrum. If he wanted to see Lady Abigail without actually courting her he'd have to go to social events she attended. Something about her made him stop and take notice. He hated it. "You're probably right." He shrugged lightly. "But that won't be any different than any other event I've attended. I think I've trained them what to expect of me don't you?"

"That is also true," George conceded. His tone less skeptical than it had been before. "But if you go, if you stay longer than you normally do they'll stop being the well trained animals you've turned them into."

Unfortunately his friend was correct. He'd have to go, seek out Lady Abigail, and then leave as fast as possible afterward. It was the only way to keep the reputation he'd carefully crafted intact. "I realize that. It's why I wasn't sure if I'd go. I'm not sure I can keep with my normal activities if I do."

"Would you like me to attend with you?" He leaned closer to the desk as he spoke. "They've come to expect you following behind me. It might make it easier for you to attend."

George would take the sting of his attendance off. They'd just assume he was with the Earl of Harrington and not question it. If he went alone he'd raise quite a few eyebrows. "You don't mind?"

"No," his friend answered. "There isn't much I wouldn't do for you. Though I do expect you to explain what you're really doing at some point. This definitely isn't out of boredom, and restlessness has never driven you to attend proper social functions."

His friend knew him too well. "When I'm ready to discuss it you'll be the first person I come to."

"Good," George said and then smiled. "We'll take my carriage. Let's start this journey to the garden party."

With that Charles and George both stood and exited the townhouse. It wasn't a far jaunt, but it would still take an hour to exit the city and then arrive at the manor house. It would be better to get on their way.

***

The Duchess of Breckenridge's garden party was a complete crush. Everyone the duchess had invited had apparently decided to attend. The only good thing about it was that the entire event was held outdoors. Otherwise Abigail would have felt as if she couldn't breathe. She really wanted to go home. If only she could get her father to agree... Instead of dwelling on something she couldn't change she decided to explore the area around the duck pond. There was a gazebo near it that she could take some respite in. So far not many guests ventured away from the gardens to explore beyond them. It was the perfect opportunity to sneak away and be alone.

She took slow measured steps so that no one took notice of her. It had been her experience that rushing away made a person stand out. Abigail had managed to slip away many times because she was ignored by everyone around her and didn't act rashly. Though some might say going off alone was foolish behavior in itself. She couldn't make herself care though. No gentleman wanted to court her and she was all right with that. Her sister could have all of their attention and hopefully Belinda would pick one to marry. At the end of the season Abigail would return to Scotland and accept her fate as a spinster. She liked books more than people anyway.

Finally she reached the gazebo and stepped inside. She leaned over the edge and stared at the pond. Several ducks swam across it and honked happily as they went around in circles. What must it be like to be a duck? They didn't seem to have a care in the world. They were happy in their watery environment and content to squawk at each other as they swam. Maybe she'd walk a little closer to the pond and get a closer view of them.

A male stepped behind her and asked, "What do you find so interesting."

Abigail nearly jumped out of her own skin at the sound of Lord Coventry's voice. He was so close she could feel his hot breath on the back of her neck. What was he doing at the duchess's garden party? Didn't he avoid these sorts of events? She'd counted on him not attending any of them. The theater had been different. It wasn't an event that was swarming with debutantes in search of a husband. "What dae ye want?"

"You wound me," he replied and held his hand over his heart. "I thought you'd be happy to see me."

"I'm not certain what gave ye that impression," she retorted. "Encouraging bad behavior on yer part was never something I wished to do."

He chuckled lightly. "But that's the best kind of behavior and I think you actually like it."

She crinkled her nose. Abigail didn't know how to answer him. He was being difficult on purpose. "I assure ye I'm always proper." Well that might not be true, but she wouldn't admit it aloud. He could think of her what he wanted to. She wasn't concerned he believed her a bit of a hellion. The truth was that she did act imprudently more often than she should. Otherwise she wouldn't have found herself alone with one of the ton's biggest rogues several times now.

He lifted a brow mockingly. "Darling," he began. "I'm not sure you comprehend the meaning of the word proper." Lord Coventry leaned even closer and whispered in her ear, "But I rather like you this way so don't change a thing."

She closed her eyes and inhaled, then exhaled slowly. His closeness played havoc on her emotions. Why did she have to like him so much? Instead of answering him she stepped away from him and out of the gazebo. She headed toward the pond to watch the ducks there. If he happened to follow she wouldn't feel so confined.

He whistled as he followed behind her. She was grateful for the sound echoing behind her. It was as if he wanted her to be aware of the progress he made. Each step that brought him closer to her made her heart beat even more heavily inside of her chest.

She stopped at the edge of the pond and tried her best to disregard Lord Coventry's presence. It was silly of her to even try. There was no ignoring a man like him. He stopped beside her. "Do you like ducks Lady Abigail?"

"I dinna mind them," she answered

"It's ironic," he said. "That I had a conversation about ducks before I came here today."

She turned to face him and said. "Oh? Why?" Why would a man such as him discuss ducks with anyone? It seemed like and odd topic of conversation.

"It wasn't about ducks exactly, more of a comparison." He grinned. "The why doesn't matter. It just struck me as funny."

He stepped closer and she took a step back on reflex and lost her balance. Her arms flailed in the air as she tried to stay upright. Lord Coventry reached for her but it was too late. Abigail fell backward and straight into the shallow end of the pond. Her skirts were soaked through and water had splashed upward drenching her bodice and some strands of her hair. This was just her luck...

"Let me help you," he insisted, but she didn't want his assistance.

She pushed him away and then he fell in beside her. Abigail glanced at earl. His fine tailored jacket and breeches were soaked through. They were a fine pair. She could either cry or laugh, she chose the latter. Her chuckles echoed around her and Lord Coventry smiled down at her. He laughed too, and it was then she realized how truly dangerous he was to her. This man could be the one male that could tempt her to fall in love. Her smile faltered, and so did his. He leaned down his lips so close to hers. The earl was going to kiss her... Should she stop him?

She decided not to. When would she have a chance to kiss a gentleman again, and she liked the idea of him being her first... His lips were warm and feather light. Almost as if they hadn't touched hers at all... Heat spread through her and she wanted to ask him to kiss her again, but she never got the chance. A duck swam behind them and let out a loud squawk.

"I suppose we should find someplace to dry off." His voice was husky as he spoke.

She nodded. "There will be gossip..."

"Let them talk," he said. "I don't mind if you don't."

Abigail chewed on her bottom lip. She didn't want to ruin her sister's chances at a good match. "But..."

"Don't worry, my lady," he said. "It will be all right. I promise."

She didn't want to think about it too long. Abigail wanted to believe him, so she chose to. If he said everything would be fine, then it would be. He stood and held out his hand to her. She placed her hand in his and he assisted her to her feet. They walked in silence back to the manor and the rest of the afternoon went by in a blur. Abigail was oblivious to the gossip around her and she did as he suggested. She put her faith in him and prayed that she wouldn't regret it.

CHAPTER 7

The dip Abigail had unwittingly taken in the pond at the Duchess of Breckenridge's garden party was not so easily forgotten as Lord Coventry thought it would be. Whispers followed her everywhere she went. They weren't exactly being covert in their discussions either. Most of them thought her the worst sort of lady and believed she was throwing herself at the earl. None of them could discern a reason why Lord Coventry could have been anywhere near that pond unless she'd lured him there. Surely she was scheming to trap the poor earl in marriage.

She snorted at that one. Lord Coventry was not a hapless fool and they were all being utterly ridiculous in their assumptions. Unfortunately, nothing she said would distract them from their way of perceiving the situation. Abigail was all but ruined because of that encounter. She didn't care for herself, but her sister didn't deserve to be ostracized. Damn Lord Coventry and his interest in her—why couldn't he have ignored her like he did other ladies?

She wanted to lean against the wall and close her eyes. To pretend, even for a few precious seconds, that the entire ton was not discussing her and what happened at the garden party, but that would be futile. In addition, it would just give the tongues in the room something else to wag about. Gossip was what made the wheels keep turning. Most of the members of the ton didn't have anything better to do and she'd given them more than enough to discuss for days to come.

The chatter came to a standstill and it the silence was almost deafening. What could have made them all stop? She turned her gaze to the entrance and fought the smile that was threatening to fill her face. Abigail should not be so happy to see Lord Coventry. He was even alone this time. Was his friend, the Earl of Harrington, unavailable to attend the ball this time? He stood at the top of the stairs that led into the ballroom and glanced around the room. Was he looking for her or someone else? Her heart skipped a beat. Abigail wanted him to be searching for her. She'd grown to anticipate his attention and enjoyed being with him.

He stopped, and glanced in her direction. Their gazes locked and his lips turned upward into a roguish smile. Her own lips tilted upward almost on their own accord. She certainly didn't smile back at him with any sense of purpose. Abigail was truly ecstatic to see him. He skipped down the stairs and pushed his way through the crown and made a beeline toward her. When he reached her he bowed slightly, then held out his hand to her. "My lady," he greeted her. That sinful smile still graced his handsome face. "May I have this dance?"

The strands of a waltz echoed through the ballroom. Other couples were already starting to fill the floor. Outside of her dance lessons she'd never actually danced the waltz with a gentleman. She nibbled on her bottom lip indecisively. She *did* want to dance—with him, and only him, but she was also suddenly nervous. What if she stepped on his toes or something equally embarrassing? Abigail didn't want to appear incapable of anything in Lord Coventry's company. Almost reluctantly she raised her hand and offered it to him. "It would be my pleasure, Lord Coventry."

He took her proffered hand and placed it in the crook of his arm and escorted her to the dance floor. Once they were in position he lead her through the dance with ease. Luckily, she hadn't stepped on his toes—yet. She fully expected to blunder eventually. She was concentrating on the steps so she didn't notice when he leaned down farther than appropriate and whispered, "I think we've skated past the point of formality don't you. Don't you think you should use by my given name now..." His hot breath caressed her ear. "Say my name, my dear. You do remember it don't you?"

Of course she did...*Charles*. He'd given her leave to use it the first time they met, but to use it was still highly inappropriate. "Thank ye but I must decline yer generous offer."

He lifted a brow and his lips tilted upward almost sardonically, then asked. "Must you?"

"Haven't ye been listening tae the rumors spreading about us already." How could he be so thickheaded? She should have declined dancing with him. It would only end up making things worse. The envious debutantes and their avaricious mothers would find a way to make her appear unfavorable some how. "It might be prudent for us to stay away from each other going forward."

"Perhaps," he began. "But I never let society dictate my actions and neither should you. It wouldn't suit either of our purposes I don't think."

"And what exactly is yer purpose my lord?" She glared at him. "Tae completely ruin whatever is left of my tattered reputation?"

"I hadn't realized you were trying to preserve it considering the first time we crossed paths you were on your way to some sort of assignation in the library at the Loxton ball."

"I was doing no such thing," she exclaimed. How dare he imply she would secretly meet a gentleman. "I only sought a few moments alone tae gather my thoughts. I dinna particularly enjoy balls and soirees. People are so...taxing." She had a sudden urge to run from the room. Tears threatened to fall and it was becoming increasingly more difficult to hold them back. Abigail had believed he thought better of her, but he was just like all the gossipmongers ripping her to shreds with their words. He actually believed her wanton and reckless. She tried to pull away from him but he held her in a firm grasp. "Let me go."

"Not yet," he replied through gritted teeth. "You will create more rumors if you flee from the middle of the dance floor. We'll finish this dance and afterward we will find some place more private to discuss this."

"As far as I'm concerned there is nothing tae discuss. Ye have said all I need tae hear."

"That's unlikely, my dear. Trust me I've left much unsaid."

She met his gaze boldly and replied, "and I've no wish tae listen tae a word. Consider our association at an end."

The strands of the music died and he brought them to a halt at the edge of the dance floor. She turned on her heels and fled from his presence. Abigail didn't run. Oh, she wanted to, but he was right. It would only make things worse and she didn't want to add any more fodder to the gossip mills. Instead she quietly, with her head held high, walked purposely to her sister and told her that she was leaving—with or without her. Luckily, Belinda didn't argue and followed her out of the ballroom. Their chaperone, bless her soul, had fallen in step behind them and didn't ask any questions. She kept the tears at bay all the way to their townhouse, but once she was in the privacy of her bedchamber they flowed freely.

Why had she fallen in love with the bloody arse?

***

Charles stared at the entrance to the Earl of Hayfield's townhouse. He had to go in there and apologize. He'd made a blunder of everything and for the first time in his life he didn't know what direction he should take. Lady Abigail would probably never want to see him ever again, and he couldn't blame her. She was right. The entire ton talked of nothing but the scene they'd created at the Duchess of Breckenridge's garden party. He had assured her that it would be all right, and for him it was. They didn't blame him for that fiasco. They'd placed the responsibility solely on Lady Abigail's delicate shoulders.

He should go inside and beg her for forgiveness. He had to make reparations in some way. If only he could figure out what would make it right. Something that would stop all the rumors...

There was only one thing that would do that—did he dare?

Charles glanced at the townhouse one last time and then spun on his heels to leave. He'd made a decision about what to do, but he needed to make a few plans first. The solution had been there all along, but he'd been too blind, and too stubborn to see it. There was a reason why he'd been drawn to Lady Abigail from the start.

He strolled down Mayfair until he reached the Earl of Harrington's home. Once there he hopped the stairs two at a time and rapped on the door. The butler opened it up and raised a bushy white eyebrow. "Lord Coventry," he greeted. "Are you expected?"

"No," he answered. "Is Lord Harrington in residence?" He hoped the answer would be in the affirmative. If he is plan was going to work he'd need his friend's assistance. Charles held a lot of sway, but as the son of a duke, George held more. Using the Duke of Southington's name would open more doors then Charles's ever would.

"He's in his study," the butler answered. "Would you like me to announce you?"

"I don't believe that will be necessary," Charles told him. "I know the way. Thank you, Bentley." He walked past the butler and went to George's study. He tapped his knuckles on the doorframe to gain his friend's attention. George had his head bent down as he studied a ledger on his desk. "I hope I'm not interrupting anything important," Charles said when George glanced up.

"Not at all," he answered. "Please come in. I could use some time away from those account books.

My head is swirling with numbers and it's causing some pain to start to throb in my temples."

Charles strolled into the room and smiled. "Then you'll be happy to put them away for the rest of the day. I need your assistance regarding Lady Abigail."

George's lips tilted upward into a wide grin. "Well, well, it's about damn time."

"How do you know what I need?" Charles lifted a brow. "I didn't even tell you what I require from you?"

His friend stood and walked over to his side. He patted Charles on the shoulder and replied, "With the rumors making the rounds? It was a matter of time you came here. If I were a betting man I'd have made a wager in the books at the club." He shook his head and chuckled lightly. "I suppose this means I can finally retire from head of the club too. You're going to need to take over if we hold you accountable to the rules. It would be a shame for you to be banned from your own club."

Charles scowled. "We'll discuss those details later. We have other things to see to first."

"That we do my friend," George agreed. "I'm assuming you'll want this done fast before you have time to talk yourself out of it. Sometimes you are you own worst enemy."

Charles didn't see it that way, but in some ways he supposed he was. It was more his own pride than anything. "I won't change my mind." Once he made a decision he didn't waver. He'd decided Lady Abigail was his the moment he met her. He just hadn't realized it until he had to face the possibility of losing her forever. "This is always where I was suppose to be, and who I was meant to find. Now it's just a matter of convincing her of the same thing."

With those words the two of them left the townhouse. As long as everything went as it should he'd be visiting Lady Abigail before the day was done.

***

Lady Abigail paced the sitting room. She was going to be ostracized and she'd be forced into hiding. Scotland wouldn't be far enough away. Her father was going to be so disappointed in her.

"Stop walking back and forth," her sister demanded. "Ye are going tae wear the carpet down."

"Listen tae ye sister," her father said as he entered the room. "There's nothing ye can dae tae change yer situation."

"Father," Abigail greeted him. "I didn't realize ye were coming tae London."

"I don't wish tae be here," he answered. He lifted her chin to force her to meet his gaze. "Yer chaperone has kept me abreast of the situation. Who is this gentleman who's been courting ye inappropriately lass?"

Lady Abigail had trouble holding her father's gaze. She'd never been so sorry for disappointing him. All she'd wanted was to make her father proud and she'd failed. It would be so nice if she could wind back the clock and redo everything. To never have gone to the library and then she'd have missed that first meeting with Lord Coventry. She wouldn't be disgraced now and having to face her father's displeasure.

"He doesn't matter," she answered. "There's nothing between us."

"On that score I disagree." The gentleman's voice echoed through the room. She had to be hearing things. Lord Coventry was not in their sitting room. Not once had he ever paid a call on her. Every meeting they'd had been at a social gathering. He strolled farther into the room and nodded at Abigail's father. "Sir," he greeted him. "I'd like permission to marry your daughter." He gestured toward. "If she'll have me."

Her father lifted a brow at her. "Dae ye want tae tie yerself tae this man? Answer now lass," he nodded at Lord Coventry. "Ye can either marry him or I can shoot him. The choice is yers."

Her mouth fell open at her father's words. Surely he wouldn't actually shoot Lord Coventry. "I'm not sure yer pistol will be necessary. It seems a bit —extreme."

"He broke yer heart didn't he?" Her father tilted his head. "Shooting him seems tae good for a bastard that plays with a lady's affections."

Lord Coventry didn't seem fazed by her father's words. "If she refuses to marry me I'll save you the trouble. I'll gladly take my own pistol to myself. There is no punishment great enough to alleviate the harm I did to your daughter's heart." He turned to Abigail and met her gaze. "It's my greatest regret that I failed you. That I botched our budding relationship with my callous disregard." He dropped to his knees before her. "If there is no faith left in me, trust me on this much. My heart beats solely for you. I've never been in love before and didn't recognize it for what it was. It surprised me more than it should have, but there it was growing inside of me with each breath, every beat of my heart, and through all the seconds I spent in your presence. Whenever we were separate you were all I could think about and I cannot imagine not spending the rest of my days without you by my side." He lifted a square cut sapphire ring up to her. "I wanted a stone to match the fire in your beautiful blue eyes, but even this doesn't manage to do them justice. Will you marry me and make me the happiest of men?"

Tears fell down her cheeks. She hadn't realized she was crying until the wetness covered them. Abigail lifted her hand to her mouth to cover the sobs that wanted to escape. Lord Coventry, no Charles, had stolen her heart and made a romantic gesture. How was she supposed to say no?

"Are ye going tae answer the lad?" her father asked. "Or dae ye plan on leaving him on his knees for eternity. I can see why ye might think he deserves it, but I'd rather toss him out the door if ye are going tae say no."

"Dinna ye dare," she told her father. She dropped to her knees and hugged the earl. "Yes, so many times yes."

"Thank God," he said and wrapped his arms around her. "I feared you might actually say no."

"Now that we've settled that we can have some refreshments," her father said. "Belinda order tea."

Her sister sighed and stood to leave. "But it was just starting tae get interesting..." she muttered more to herself than anyone else as she exited the sitting room.

Charles stood and then helped Abigail to her feet as well. "I have a special license," Charles said. "Harrington helped me get it. We can get married today if you wish."

"Ye will not have a hasty wedding as if my daughter has something tae hide." Her father glared at him. "The banns will be read proper and ye will be married in a church."

Charles nodded. "As you wish. May I have a moment alone with your daughter."

"No," her father answered. "Ye have had tae many moments alone with her as it is from what I've been told."

Abigail shouldn't laugh but the expression on Charles's face was not one she'd forget anytime soon. He wasn't used to being denied anything. "We'll have time tae ourselves later. After all we do have a wedding tae plan."

He smiled and kissed her cheek. Her father glowered, but if he didn't like it he should have given them the time Charles had requested. "You're right of course. We have our whole lives to enjoy time by ourselves. We can certainly humor your father now."

At the start of her day she'd never dreamed at the end of it she'd be happier than she'd ever been in her life. Now she was affianced to the man she loved beyond all reason, and soon she'd be his wife. Marriage was never something she'd wanted for herself, but sometimes life took unexpected turns. Meeting Charles had altered her course and she nothing would make her regret that she had found him. Love made everything worthwhile.

EPILOGUE

London, 1808

Charles shook off the rain that had settled over his jacket but it didn't help. He was soaked through and through. The gloominess of the day fit his mood. Grief overwhelmed him and he needed to hug his wife, and then his daughter in that order. The funeral of his dear friend, George, the Earl of Harrington had nearly destroyed him. Seeing the devastation on George's son's face had brought him even lower. Poor, poor Jonas—he'd lost his mother and his father in the same day. One to death and the other to fear... The Duke of Southington would never have allowed his grandson to be left in the care of Sarah, the Countess of Harrington. Southington would consider her too weak to raise the future duke.

"Are ye all right," Abigail asked. He pulled her into his arms and kissed the top of her head. They'd been married for almost eight years now. His wife and daughter were the light of his life. Without them he'd be lost. It was hard to believe he'd thought he'd never fall in love. It had changed him in so many ways.

"I'm not," he answered. "But I will be. Is Marian awake?"

"She's with nanny in the nursery. It is almost time for her nap." Their daughter was four years old and completely precocious. She had her mother's auburn hair and Charles's green eyes. To him she was a perfect blend of the two of them. "But if ye go now ye can take over from nanny. Marian always like's yer stories."

He kissed Abigail one more time and then headed to the nursery. Marian jumped when he entered and ran to him. "Daddy," she said gleefully. "You tell me a story."

The little hellion was demanding, but he loved her so much his heart nearly burst with it. "I might be persuaded to." He nodded at the nanny. "You can take a break. I'll put her down for her nap."

"Very well, my lord," the nanny answered and exited the room.

He carried Marian over to her bed and laid her down, then pulled her favorite blanket over her. "Now what kind of story would you like?"

"Princess," she demanded.

"Ah, you want a story about yourself do you?" He brushed her auburn locks away from her eyes. "Those are my favorite kind too, but I think today we'll add a prince too."

"No, just me."

"Prince's need love sometimes too. This one is especially sad. He's not as lucky as you are. You have both your mommy and daddy, but the prince has lost everyone who loves him."

She pushed her lip out in a pout, but didn't stop him from continuing the story. His little princess had a big heart and it would only grow more empathetic as she aged. She was more like her mother in that regard.

"He's had a hard life. Much harsher than any prince should ever have and growing up without love will only make him push people away."

"Like mommies and daddies?" Marian asked.

"Those that would help guide him and help him open himself up to love. It might take the love of a special person to help him find happiness again." Charles had decided he'd be there for Jonas as he grew, but a part of him wondered if perhaps a union between his daughter, and his best friend's son might be in their future. Only time would tell if that was possible.

"Like a princess?" Marian supplied after he was quiet for longer than she liked.

"A very special princess will help heal his heart. One day you might be the one to help heal his sadness." He kissed her head. "Now it's time to sleep little one."

"Love you, daddy," she whispered as her eyes fluttered closed. He stood and stared down at her as she slipped into dreamland. She would always be his little princess. As far as Jonas, the new Earl of Harrington, he'd do his best to help the young lord. He'd need someone to help guide him that didn't rule him with an iron fist like the Duke of Southington, and if should fate deem it, maybe Jonas and Marian would be destined to find love together too. He rather liked the idea of George's son being formally a part of his family...

EXCERPT: WHEN AN EARL TURNS WICKED

BLUESTOCKINGS DEFYING ROGUES
BOOK ONE

DAWN BROWER

Dawn Brower

When an Earl
Turns Wicked

PROLOGUE

Southington Castle, England, 1808

The day was like any other one in England. Rainfall had become a normal enough occurrence that Jonas didn't notice it—even as it dripped down his face, drenching him completely. He stared at the chiseled stones in the cemetery near Southington's chapel. Only members of his family were buried there—many he never met personally. Pictures of them filled the great hall, but they were history to him, and he'd been able to distance himself from their stories. This, however, was far different.

His life would never be the same. The death of his father had marked an unchangeable truth. The duke now had control over Jonas's life. His grandfather was a tyrant and had always attempted to browbeat his will into him. His father had been the one person he'd been able to count on. A buffer the duke couldn't break through, and he'd tried often.

So, no, the cold didn't matter because he was numb through and through. Rain? Paltry in comparison to what he had yet to face. The Duke of Southington, his grandfather, hadn't started yet—mainly because he couldn't. There were people around, and he dared not cause a scene. Once all the mourners departed, things would start to unravel ever further around him. Would his grandfather allow him to return to Eton? What about his mother? Would she have it in her to fight him? Somehow, he doubted everything and yet prayed for anything resembling his life before his father's death.

"Lord Harrington," a man said as he rested his hand on Jonas's shoulder. How could *he* be the earl now? That was his father's name, and he doubted he'd ever become accustomed to it. "It's time to head back."

He glanced up at the man as the rain continued to drip down his face. His hair was black, but had already started to turn to gray along the sides. Jonas barely knew him, but Lord Coventry had been a friend of his father's. "I'm not ready," he told him.

"George was a good man," Lord Coventry said. "He loved you."

"I know," Jonas replied woodenly. He'd long ago stopped feeling and now went through the motions. What else could he do? Lord Coventry was correct—it was long past time to go, yet he couldn't move. Once he left, it would all become too real for him. His grandfather would start barking orders, and he had years before he could be free of him. Three long years to be exact—once he turned eighteen he could seize control of his inheritance. As long as his grandfather didn't find a way to break the will. "But that doesn't change anything."

"No," Lord Coventry agreed. "He's still gone, and nothing will ever bring him back."

If Jonas were capable of crying, he'd have done so days ago. It was probably a good thing he hadn't. Any sign of weakness would have set his grandfather off. He had to be brave, and somehow find the strength to move on sooner than he'd like. His father deserved to be mourned, but he'd understand why Jonas couldn't openly do it. "I'm ready now." Jonas didn't look at Lord Coventry. He spun on his heels and began the long trek back to Southington Castle. He hated his grandfather's home—it was as cold as he was. There wasn't anything welcoming about it.

"Lord Harrington—"

"Don't call me that," Jonas interrupted. The sound of his father's title shot pain through his already aching heart. He didn't want to think or feel. Everything reminded him of his father and the loss that he couldn't escape. The title... That was more than he could bear.

Lord Coventry cleared his throat. "It's who you are now."

"That may be." Jonas swallowed hard. "But filling my father's shoes is something I'm not yet prepared for. I can't hear his title without thinking of him and what I've lost."

"I understand," Coventry said and sighed. "You're too young to have lost your father already. If I had a son..." He shook his head. "That doesn't matter. You have a long road ahead of you, and there's probably no one you feel you can trust. You might not know it yet, but you can trust me." He paused for a moment before continuing, "What would you like me to call you?"

"Nothing," Jonas said. "I doubt we will see each other again after today."

The older man laughed. It was a foreign sound, considering their surroundings. Sadness permeated everything around them, yet the earl had found something humorous. Coventry seemed like a likeable sort and in another time, Jonas may have liked him. Somehow, he doubted he'd find anything appealing or even joyous for a long time.

Coventry gestured toward the castle in the distance. "We shall see. Come, let's get out of this rain."

The earl followed behind Jonas as they entered the castle. He didn't stay long after that. He'd spoken to the duke quietly before his departure, and the duke didn't argue or order the earl around. That alone made Jonas wonder what they'd discussed.

"Now that everyone is gone we have some things to discuss, boy." His grandfather stormed across the room and glared down at him. "Starting with your education... I was going to keep you here, but Coventry made a good point. You'll need to make connections, and those are rooted in school. So, I'll allow you to return to Eton—at least for the rest of this school year. We'll revisit that idea before the next term."

He owed the earl far more than he realized. Never had he truly believed his grandfather would allow him to return to school. "Thank you."

"Don't thank me yet," his grandfather said

gruffly. "We have a lot of work ahead of us to prepare you for the dukedom."

He was barely an earl, and now he had to worry about grandfather's title? Jonas wanted to curl up into a ball and sleep for days—no, weeks. That was the cowardly way though, and he refused to give in to it. "Where is Mother?"

"She's gone to live with her sister," he replied. "Your mother is too delicate for Southington. Don't worry. Your father made sure she'd be provided for."

His mother had abandoned him? He'd always been closer to his father, but still... She left him alone with the duke, and she was well aware of his brutish nature. He had no problems using his fists to make a point. The Harrington title was prestigious, but he wouldn't have control of the estate for many years. They had plenty of funds as long as they did what the duke wanted. His father had decided to cut as many ties as possible with Southington. They lived in a small townhouse in London, and his father had invested in a profitable shipping company with the income he had available. They didn't live in splendor, but they'd been comfortable.

None of it had made the duke happy, but then nothing could. He liked having control over his family, and losing it had made him cut them out of his life. That was until his father died and he saw a way to wiggle his way back in. Now, Jonas was his ward until he gained full access to his inheritance. It was not a huge sum, but it would be enough for him to break free.

"May I be excused?" The duke hit Jonas's mouth with his fist before he was fully prepared for its impact. Jonas jerked backward involuntarily, but then gained control as quick as possible. He lifted his gaze and stared the duke in the eye, repeating his request, "May I be excused now?" Leaving without permission would prolong the torture, and he didn't want another punch to the face, or anywhere else.

The duke nodded, and Jonas left as fast as his feet would carry him. He didn't run as he wanted to because he would not give in to the duke's bullying. If he darted out of the room, his grandfather would find a reason to make him stay. Instead, he walked briskly and steadily until he reached his chambers. Only then, once the door was closed and he had privacy, did he give in to the emotions raging through him. The tears he'd held in finally flowed freely, and he grieved for his father.

C

London, 1812

JONAS PICKED UP THE GLASS OF BRANDY ON THE table and took a drink. He set it back down and stared at the cards in his hand. So far, luck hadn't been on his side, and he was steadily losing what funds he had. He should have given up a long time ago but stupidly thought he'd win if he kept playing. Freedom had led him astray when it should have brought him happiness. He learned fast that the latter was an elusive emotion not meant for him.

"I think it's time to call it a night," announced Jason Thompson, Earl of Asthey. He ran his fingers through his dark blond hair and grinned like a cat that'd caught the prize mouse. "It's been a productive night."

At least it was going well for one of them. "I'm ready too." He threw his cards on the table. "I've lost too much as it is." And he had very little he could afford to lose. His grandfather still held onto most of the purse strings. Somehow, the duke had found a way to gain control over a large part of his inheritance. Jonas had won his independence a year ago, but he wasn't truly free. The one thing he had left that the duke couldn't touch was a tiny sum his maternal grandmother had left him. It barely gave him enough to live on. He needed to figure out how to raise his income, but he was at a loss on how.

"That's a shame," Asthey said. "Winning big would solve a lot of your woes."

Jonas rolled his eyes. "I need more than I'd win in a few hands of cards to solve all that." It might help if his grandfather decided to roll over and die, but no, that wouldn't happen. The old man was too bullheaded to do anything as congenial as save the world from his type of meanness. "Where is Shelby?" Gregory Cain, the Earl of Shelby, was the other member of their trio. Jonas scanned the room for Shelby's midnight locks. They were his trademark. No one else had hair quite as sinfully dark as his. His friend was nowhere to be seen in the gaming hell.

"He found a light-skirt to his liking and appropriated a room for a bit of sport."

Of course he did... Shelby was quite the rake, and relished in ravishing any willing female in his vicinity. "Should we wait?"

"He knows his way home," Asthey replied. "I rather not wait on him to finish. He might take all night, or he could come out in an hour. It's hard to say with him."

"You're right," Jonas agreed. He stood and pulled

on his jacket and buttoned it over his waistcoat. "I'm tired and would rather sleep in my own bed."

They both headed to the front door and exited the gaming hell. It was still quite dark, and for once it was a rather clear night in London. The rain had been dreadful for days. The streets were filled with puddles and mud. They walked in silence for a few moments as they headed for a nearby hackney. As they stepped onto the road to cross over to the carriage, Jonas was yanked backward. He fell to the ground, his head smacking against the hard surface.

"Bloody hell," he said with a groan. "Why'd you do that?"

"I have a message for you." A big, burly man loomed over Jonas.

Jonas lifted a brow. "You might want to work on your delivery. I won't be recommending your service to anyone."

"Don't need it," the burly man replied. Jonas couldn't make out his features in the dark, but felt the sting of a fist hitting his jaw. "The message isn't the verbal kind."

Jonas was poised to throw another punch, but was jerked backward before he could land it. The man hit the ground in much the same manner as Jonas had. Served the bastard right... Jonas leapt to his feet before the other man could get up. He rubbed his hand over his sore jaw. "Took you long enough." He turned to whom he'd thought was Asthey, but was shocked to find Lord Coventry instead.

"Where's Asthey?"

"There." Coventry pointed in the distance. He was battling a ruffian of his own. He landed a solid blow, and the man fell to the ground. "What is going on?"

"Unfortunately, this is the work of your grandfather," he replied. A hint of sadness echoed through his voice. "I heard a rumor and came to investigate the veracity of it."

"And?" Jonas didn't like where this conversation was going. His grandfather could do a lot of damage if he wanted to, and it appeared as if he'd decided to employ his power. He had to have all the information Coventry possessed so he could form a plan of his own. His grandfather's contacts were extensive and his reach even farther. In order to beat him at his own game Jonas might have to fight dirty.

"I'm afraid it was correct by the looks of things," Coventry answered.

Asthey joined them, shaking his hand in the air as he walked. "That hurts more than I want to admit.

I might need to learn a thing or two about throwing a proper punch."

Coventry nodded. "I might be able to help you both." He turned to Asthey. "Go inside and fetch your friend, Shelby. I have a proposition for you all."

Asthey didn't question Coventry's order. He nodded and headed back into the gaming hell. Jonas watched him until he disappeared inside, and then turned back to Coventry. "What do you know?"

"Far more than you do," he replied cryptically. "The duke has plans for you, and he's not happy with your reluctance to follow them."

"That's something I know far too well." He wished the old man would leave him alone already. "Was this his way of forcing me to go to Southington?"

"I'm not entirely sure what he hoped to accomplish tonight," Coventry admitted. "I know he arranged it, and I'm here to help if you'll allow it."

Jonas was so tired of constantly fighting with his grandfather. There had to be a way to stop him from coming after him again and again. "What do you have in mind?"

Asthey and Shelby came out of the gaming hell and joined them. Shelby carried his cravat in his hand and was straightening his jacket. "This better be important," Shelby muttered. "The chit was..."

"We don't need to know," Asthey said, interrupting him.

Coventry smiled. "I believe you boys will fit right in."

"I don't follow," Jonas said, then frowned. "Fit in where?"

"A very special club," he replied. "Come along. I'll explain everything and how it'll help you with Southington, your social life, and even financially, if you like."

He didn't understand how a club could do all that, but he was willing to hear Coventry out. He had saved him from being beaten, and as long as Jonas had his two friends with him, he didn't see the harm. They could decide together if it was something worth doing. They'd stuck together this long.

They followed Coventry to a nearby carriage and climbed inside. It rolled across the cobbled street with ease. The interior was plush, and the seats rather comfortable. Jonas had never ridden in a carriage so fine. After a short drive, the carriage stopped. They all got outside to find an elegant townhouse with a W emblazoned near the door.

Where were they? What had Coventry said earlier? Something about a club.

"Where are we?" Asthey asked vocalizing Jonas's thoughts.

"Doesn't look like much," Shelby replied. "Why'd I leave that lovely lass again?"

Coventry pulled a key out of his pocket that had the same W on the top of it. He pushed it into the lock and opened the door." "Gentleman, please come inside." He led them from the foyer into the main part of the house.

The outside expertly disguised the decadence found inside. Rich velvet draped the windows. The settees, chaise lounge, and every chair in the place had similar color scheme of dark red and burnished brown. To the side was a long cherry banister that wound around an elaborate staircase. To the side was a large room with a blazing fireplace. Several men sat at one of the tables as they played cards. Each one had a beautiful, scantily clad woman on their lap. Jonas's mouth fell open at everything he saw, and he couldn't believe he didn't know the place existed. He turned to Coventry and said, "You have our attention. Want to explain this to us now?" He continued to stare at the luxuriousness of his surroundings.

Coventry smiled. "Welcome to the club. You have been nominated for admission—if you want to join. There are rules, of course," Coventry told them. "Nothing too extreme, but you should all find them reasonable. Keep the club a secret, and you forfeit your membership once you marry—only the leader of the group is allowed to have a wife and retain his membership. If you're wondering who that is—I am the currently in charge of the club and its members." He glanced at each one of them and asked, "Do you wish to be a part of all this?" He held his arms out wide.

They all nodded immediately. Jonas didn't give it much thought, and figured the other two hadn't either. The sheer excess of the place had won them over. The rest he could figure out later.

It was a decision he never regretted...

CHAPTER 1

London, 1823

Dark gray clouds floated in the sky above, threatening to unleash rain upon everyone who dared to walk the streets of London. Lady Marian Lindsay stared up at them as she chewed her bottom lip. It was not a good sign, and she hoped the bad omen didn't lead to a disastrous meeting with Sir Anthony Davis. Not that rain wasn't commonplace in England—because it most certainly graced the country with regularity; however, Marian's luck never held when it deigned to fall from the sky. So her meeting with Sir Anthony would surely be doomed.

Nonetheless, she fully intended to go through with it. She had plans, and Sir Anthony stood in the way of them. Without his permission, she'd never become a part of the Royal Medical Society. They had this misbegotten notion medicine and women didn't mix. She hoped to change his mind and have him recommend her for admission.

She'd been studying medicine and herbs her entire life. All right, maybe not that long, but it felt like it. Her interest started almost a decade ago after her aunt and uncle's death. They'd both been in a terrible carriage accident near her family estate. Her father was the Earl of Coventry. Her uncle, the Earl of Frossly, married her Aunt Belinda and became a part of the family. After their death, Marian's mother had been desperate with grief and the loss of her beloved younger sister.

Everything in Marian's life changed after that. Her two cousins came to live with them, and her mother became sick following their arrival—leaving her launch into society, as well as her cousin's, forgotten. Not that she had minded especially once her mother succumbed to her illness and they lost her forever. Her grief had been too great, and she'd decided she wanted more in life. Marian didn't want to marry and have children. She had much loftier goals—like becoming an actual physician and making a living helping people.

Which brought her back to Sir Anthony—he had to let her into the society. This was the next step to gaining the knowledge she needed to become a doctor. She glanced up at the sky once more.

"Please hold off until I'm done," she begged. "I need a little bit of time." She quickened her pace until she reached Sir Anthony's building and pushed the door open. Marian entered as the rain started to fall. It pounded against the street, creating puddles almost instantly. She shut the door and blew out a relieved breath.

Someone cleared their throat. She turned and found two men standing inside, staring at her with a modicum of surprise etched on their faces. The older gentleman must have been Sir Anthony. He had dark hair streaked with gray. The other gentleman was rather handsome—dashing even. He had dark hair and devilish blue eyes. Much to her chagrin, she'd always found him enticing, and not because he was the most gorgeous male she'd ever seen. There was something about him that made the heart inside her chest beat heavily. Marian's whole body hummed with some unnamable energy. Jonas Parker, the esteemable Earl of Harrington, would always put her at a disadvantage, and sometimes she believed he knew it too. *Damn him.* "Hello, my lord," Marian greeted him and then turned to the older man. "Sir Anthony." She hoped her presumption was correct and he was the man she thought, or wouldn't that be embarrassing...

"Lady Marian," Lord Harrington said in a slow drawl. "Does your father know you're in this part of town?"

Drat. Of course that would be the first thing he'd ask—at least he hadn't corrected her about Sir Anthony. "My father is well aware of my activities." That wasn't entirely a lie. He did know she hoped to be a doctor and humored her. He didn't really believe she'd succeed, but she planned on proving him wrong. Men had all the advantages in society and women were given little say in their lives. Something she hated to the depths of her soul. "You needn't worry about me."

"What may we assist you with?" Sir Anthony asked. "Did the rain drive you inside?"

Lord Harrington lifted a brow. "I don't think that's it at all." He kept his gaze on Marian, unnerving her. He saw too much, and she rather disliked the scrutiny. "You're here because of your little project, aren't you?"

Anyone acquainted with her father, and therefore her, was aware of her desire to be a doctor. Her father boasted of her hobby even though he doubted her. It was his way of giving her his support. Not that it was a lot or even a stamp of approval, but it had managed to aid her in her quest thus far. "What if I am?" She jutted out her chin. "You aim to prevent me from taking the next step?"

He held out his hands in front of him. "Far be it from me to step in front of a bluestocking on a mission. By all means, say your piece and see if Sir Anthony is willing to assist you."

Sir Anthony glanced back and forth between them, but Marian barely noticed. She was irritated more than she should be. Lord Harrington was being nice by allowing her to speak—a sardonic, arrogant, and presumptuous...*man*. Rolling her eyes would not help her convince Sir Anthony she should be a part of the Royal Medical Society. She took a deep breath to calm herself. Calling him names inside her head would not further her goals. She had to pull herself together and try to present herself in the best light to Sir Anthony.

"You require something from me?" Anthony asked as he gave her his full attention. "What is it?"

"Well," she started. This was much harder than she thought it would be. "I have a request I hope you'll agree to."

"Oh?"

That was it. Nothing else from him or any encouragement for her to go on. Lord Harrington, the rogue, leaned against a nearby table and crossed his arms over his chest. He had a wicked grin on his too handsome face. If Marian wasn't a lady, she'd do something to wipe that knowing smile away. Someone should put him in his place, and maybe then he wouldn't be so condescending.

"I've been studying for a while to be a physician..."

"You have?" Sir Anthony scrunched his eyebrows together. "Your father knows you're doing this?"

"Well, yes," she said. "I did mention he was aware of my activities..."

"She's a bluestocking," Lord Harrington added. "You know how they are when they get an idea in their head. It's why I didn't stop her when she came in, if you'll recall."

Marian gave in and rolled her eyes. She couldn't

help herself any longer. Why did she have to be attracted to him? He drove her mad in more ways than she could count, yet he was the one man her body became alive near. She hated him for it. "Thank you, my lord." She pasted a cheerful smile on her face. "You give glowing recommendations."

"It's the least I can do," he replied with that sinful voice of his. It sent shivers down her spine. "As you can see, Sir Anthony is quite scandalized with your chosen hobby. He's gone mute with the shock of it."

Damn him, he was right. Sir Anthony stared at her as if she were a bug to be studied in length. He hadn't said a word in several heartbeats. "I had hoped you'd foster my admission into the Royal—"

"Absolutely not," he responded with vehemence. "Ladies do not become doctors or study anything. I don't understand this generation and their need to poke their noses in things they best not be a part of."

"Some ladies find science and knowledge enticing," Marian said as she lifted her head in defiance. "Intelligence is quite an attractive asset to inspire to."

"Touché," Lord Harrington agreed. "But I'd take it a step further and suggest there are things a gentleman finds more attractive in a lady than what's inside their head."

She shook her head. "I didn't come here to debate the qualities one looks for in a potential spouse. I want to become an active member of the Royal Medical Society."

"That's not going to happen, my dear. I'm afraid women are not allowed and never will be." Sir Anthony squared his shoulders, preparing for battle. Good, she planned on giving him something to fight about.

"Never is a long time to adhere to," Lady Marian replied. "Do you want to limit yourself when there are infinite possibilities if you'd open yourself up to them?"

"It's not up to me," Sir Anthony told her. "Society has rules for a reason. Go home and do something more ladylike. It truly is for the best."

She narrowed her gaze and pursed her lips together. *Ladylike?* He was much worse than Lord Harrington. At least the earl pretended to give her the space to argue her stance. Sir Anthony was an old-fashioned sycophant. He thought playing up to her feminine tributes would make her abandon her calling and do a bit of embroidery instead. Why could a man do anything he wanted, but a woman had inadequate options? If she decided to take up water colors or the pianoforte, they'd encourage her. Being a doctor though? That was a ridiculous notion.

"Thank you for your sage advice," Marian replied with false sweetness. "I'll leave you gentleman to whatever you were discussing. It's time for me to return home. Good day." She curtsied and turned to the door.

"Wait," Lord Harrington demanded as he stepped forward. "I'll escort you."

"There's no need," she explained. Marian did not want him following her home. If he spoke to her father, then much more than a failed attempt to gain entry into the Royal Medical Society would befall her. "I managed to arrive here safely without an escort. I don't need one to see I find my way home."

"Perhaps," he replied cordially. "But I will be by your side every step of the way regardless. I'd never forgive myself if something happened to you and I could have prevented it." The corner of his mouth lifted enticingly. "I admire your father, and for that alone I'd see you safely to the ends of the Earth. Nothing you can say will talk me out of this."

Damn him. She cursed him for the thousandth time in the space of a half hour. At that rate, she'd start saying it aloud. There was no way she'd win in an argument with him. The easiest way would be to agree, but that irritated her nonetheless.

"Fine," she replied. "Have it your way."

"I always do," he retorted. "Good of you to see that." His blue eyes practically twinkled with mischief. He was a conceited scoundrel.

She ground her teeth together and refrained from responding. Instead, she spun on her heels and exited the building and Sir Anthony's misogyny. She would not give up on her dream. There had to be another way, and if there was, she'd find it.

The rain hadn't stopped while she was inside the shop. It beat against her in a rapid staccato, making her wish she'd stayed inside a bit longer, or procured a carriage. Why hadn't she planned this a little better? Because that would have made sense... She'd been blinded by her ambition and the need to be a part of something much bigger than herself. One day she'd learn the benefit of a well laid plan. Unfortunately, that day was not this one.

"Come with me," Lord Harrington leaned down and spoke directly into her ear. His heat enveloped her, making her forget where she was for a moment. He picked up her hand and rested it on his arm to lead her in the direction of his choosing. "My carriage is around the corner."

She blinked several times as rain continued to drown out the sound of the London Street. What was happening to her? She shook her head and did as Lord Harrington said. A carriage in this kind of weather was desirable, and for the first time since she saw him inside Sir Anthony's place, she was happy to have him near.

Thankfully, Lord Harrington's carriage wasn't far away. He helped her inside, but unfortunately, she was already soaked through. She couldn't wait to return home and put some distance between them. Uncomfortable wasn't a strong enough word to describe how he made her feel, and it didn't help that she was drenched from head to toe. She had to look a fright... What nonsense.

Why did she care if she looked less than desirable? Lord Harrington wasn't a potential suitor even if she was looking for a husband. He was one of the biggest rogues of the ton, and she was firmly on the shelf. Marian was a bluestocking and a spinster in the making, as untouchable as possible and quite content with that fate. Her pent up wantonness could dwindle down to nothing. She didn't need a man to find happiness.

Maybe she'd found a spot of luck in a sea of bad fortune. So, she'd taken a couple steps backward from her main goal. That didn't mean she couldn't find a way to move forward. For now, she'd allow Lord Harrington to see her home, and then she'd meet with her two closest friends to make a new plan. This was not the end of anything. Marian chose to see to it as a beginning. The likes of Sir Anthony and Lord Harrington would not discourage her.

EXCERPT: ODDS OF LOVE

SCANDAL MEETS LOVE

Scandal Meets Love

Odds of
Love

USA TODAY BESTSELLING AUTHOR
Dawn Brower

PROLOGUE

January 1816

S now trickled down from the sky and blanketed the ground. Lady Katherine Wilson pulled her cloak tighter around her and did her best to suppress a shiver. The frigid temperature managed to seep underneath the wool cloak and spread over her. She wanted desperately to reach her destination and escape from the cold. She hated winter. It had never been her favorite time of year, and today was no different. It would be better if she could stay home and sit in front of the fire in the sitting room. Even Fortuna's Parlor would be preferable. To be fair each day since her grandmother passed away had been dismal though. What she didn't want to do was visit with solicitors and discuss her loss in depth. Her grandmother was gone. Hadn't she suffered enough already?

She finally reached the offices of her grandmother's solicitor and stepped up to the doorway, and knocked. Katherine had never been to a solicitor before and had no clue what to do. What exactly was the proper protocol when dealing with a solicitor? The finishing school she'd attended hadn't prepared her for this particular circumstance. She probably could have asked Narissa or even Diana, but she hadn't wanted to burden them with her troubles.

The door opened and an older gentleman filled the entryway. He had dark hair with salt and pepper strands streaked through the sides. His dark waistcoat gave him a somber appearance that reflected in his ice blue eyes. Something about him seemed familiar but Katherine couldn't place him in her memory. "Lady Katherine," he greeted her. "Please come in out of the cold."

Had she met him previously? How had he known her at a glance? She would have to inquire during their meeting. "Mr. Adamson?" Katherine lifted a brow. She wanted to make sure he was the solicitor she had to a meeting with.

"Yes," he answered as he gestured her past the doorway and closed it behind her.

Katherine shivered. The cold hadn't quite left her even with the warmth that already enveloped her. Sadly, after the conference she'd have to walk home in the awful weather. She really wished a carriage had been available to her, but her mother had used it to pay calls.

"Can I take your cloak?" Mr. Adamson asked.

She wanted to keep it on because she was still a little cold; however, soon it would be too warm and it was better to take it off now. Besides she wasn't sure how long their conversation would take. Katherine shrugged the cloak off and handed it to him. He placed it on a nearby hook and then turned toward her. "Follow me. You'll be more comfortable in the office. There's a fire in the hearth and its much warmer."

Mr. Adamson led her to the office and gestured toward a chair. He sat behind a desk and shuffled some papers before glancing back at her. "You're probably wondering why I asked you to meet me here. Normally I'd conduct a visit such as this one in the comfort of the client's home. But because of the nature of your grandmother's last wishes I'm required to do it here. She was afraid that if we met at your father's home he'd try to take control of the assets she left to you. Not that he could have..." He cleared his throat and then continued, "But this makes things simpler for you. There is no conflict to deal with and once you leave you will have control of your inheritance."

What could her grandmother have left for her? She thought her father had inherited all of her grandmother's possessions. Not that Katherine expected he to have much. Most of the estate had already gone to her father when his father passed. It was part of the entailment. Her grandmother lived in a house in Sussex county, near Heathfield. She had always assumed it was the dower house though... "I am not certain I understand."

He handed her a letter. "It is all explained here. You're a very wealthy young lady."

Katherine took the missive from him and broke the seal. "It's from my grandmother..." She recognized her handwriting immediately. Her heart beat heavily in her chest and she fought the urge to cry. She'd been letting her sadness getting the best o her for longer than she would have liked. Katherine missed her grandmother terribly.

"Keep reading," Mr. Adamson encouraged her. "It's important you read it until the end."

Katherine turned her attention back to her grandmother's words. What could she have had to say that she couldn't say before she passed away?

My Dearest Grandchild,

Your heart must be heavy, and I'm sorry for the pain you are now feeling. If I could take all your hurt away I would, but if you're reading this then I must no longer be with you. My death, while painful, gives you freedom in ways you probably never imagined. My son, your father, is a harsh man and has not given you the love you need. He learned his behaviors from his own father. My marriage was an arranged one and my mother made assurances that I'd always be provided for. In England, property is immediately owned by a woman's husband after marriage vows are said.

My mother didn't believe a woman should be controlled by a man. Love isn't the main requirement in marriage and often doesn't play a part in the contract settlements. That was the case with my own nuptials. A Dukedom such as Gladstone was forged on the bonds of many unions. John was destitute and agreed to all the contractual stipulations before I married him. It was never my desire to become a duchess, but it made my father practically salivate, but I digress.

The important thing you need to understand is that I was never a pawn, and you don't need to be either. My money was controlled by me, but a generous sum was bestowed upon John after we said our vows. He had his money, and I had mine. I provided him with his heir and after that we lived separate lives. Luckily, John didn't waste his money and rebuilt the Gladstone estates. Charles is more his son than mine. Don't let him control you. Seize control of your life.

There are so many things I want to say to you, but the most important last words I can leave you with is this. Marry for love and nothing more. My estate is yours. Use it wisely, my dear. I trust you will make the right decisions. You have the ability to choose your own path now. Happiness can be yours, and love as well.

All my love,

Grandmother

Katherine wiped a tear from her cheek. Her father wasn't always hard, but she understood what her grandmother meant. Her father wanted to control everything and everyone around him. He hated to be thwarted.

Katherine glanced at Mr. Adamson and asked, "What exactly did my grandmother leave me?"

"As the letter states—her entire estate," he responded matter-of-factly.

"I understand, but what does her estate entail?" She repressed the urge to roll her eyes. "She says I'm wealthy now. Does she mean I have unlimited funds?"

"You do have a sizeable bank account now. There is approximately ten thousand pounds in her account," he answered. "She also left you a horse farm in Sussex. That was your grandmother's main estate and she had a cottage near Bath that you now own. The farm brings in around five thousand pounds per annum"

Katherine's mouth fell open. That was a lot of money... She could do anything she wanted just as her grandmother said in her letter, but Katherine hadn't fully appreciated her words until she heard what she'd inherited. "And my father can't take it away from me?" It was a concern because her father didn't like anyone having more than he did. She couldn't say the state of the dukedom, but that amount of money would surely rival it. He would want it and control of the farm.

"No," he said. "The contracts were clear. Any money she had could only be given to a direct female relation of hers. The only way your father would have inherited it would have been if there were no females to inherit." He lifted his lips upward. "Even then, the first female born of her direct bloodline would gain control of the assets. A male can only retain guardianship of it until a female is born. It's a matriarchal estate."

There were so many possibilities available to her. She wasn't sure what she should do first. Never in her wildest dreams would she have foreseen this happening. Her grandmother's death was the worst and best thing that had ever happened to her. Why hadn't she told her that she'd inherit so much from her? Did she think it would have made a difference in their relationship? Her grandmother had always meant so much to her.

"Is there anything I need to do?" Katherine's mind was still reeling from the news. "Can I go to the farm?"

Her grandmother had always visited her. She'd

never been to her estate in Sussex. Katherine had a sudden desire to be amongst her things and the place she loved. It might help her feel closer to her grandmother again. It might be silly, but she needed it.

"There is nothing required of you. Everything has been put into your name. There's nothing you need to do but accept your inheritance. If you require anything please let me know and I'll see to it." He slid a stack of papers toward her. "These are for your records. I keep a copy here if they're ever lost and yes, to answer your question, you may visit the farm. If you so desire, you may relocate to Sussex permanently. There's no reason for you to remain at the ducal estate or under your father's care."

That settled it for her. She would go home and pack, then set off for the farm in Sussex. Traveling in winter wasn't her favorite, but to be away from her father would be a blessing. She didn't tell even her closest friends how horrible he could be. Diana and Narissa had no idea how hard it could be for her to sneak out of the house or even to openly gain permission to attend a function. She didn't live the happy-go-lucky life they believed she did. The main reason she'd been looking for a husband was to escape her father's control. Now she didn't have to marry unless she wanted to. She was free to live her life and not worry about anything ever again.

"Thank you so much." Katherine came to her feet. "How soon can I travel there?"

"I can have a carriage ready to take you at any time. When do you wish to go?" He stood and walked around the desk to her side. "The servants already are aware of your ownership and expect you to visit. They're anxious to meet you. They all loved your grandmother."

"I'd like to go at first light tomorrow." Katherine couldn't wait to meet the servants. If they loved her grandmother as she did they'd have much to discuss. "Is that too soon?"

"Not at all," he reassured her. "I'll have a carriage readied. Do you require a chaperone or are you taking your maid with you."

Betty would love to accompany her. She was the only servant in her father's household solely loyal to Katherine. "My maid will be with me." They exited his office and Mr. Adamson retrieved her cloak, then assisted her with it.

"Very well then." He smiled down at her. Where he'd seemed cold to her before he now seemed— almost fatherly, or at least how she imagined a father should be. "Don't forget to let me know if you require anything of me. Safe travels on your journey. I believe you will be pleasantly surprised by the farm. It's a wonderful place. I've visited there often on business for your grandmother."

She'd already thanked him, but it didn't seem like enough. He'd changed her life in the span of less than an hour. Yes, it really was her grandmother that had made her life more bearable, but Mr. Adamson was bearer of that bright news. "I'm sure I'll be fine; however, if something does arise I'll be sure to inform you. Have a good day." Katherine nodded to him and then exited the solicitor's office. For the first time in weeks she walked home with a smile, and not once, even in thought, did she grumble about the cold.

EXCERPT: CHANCE OF LOVE

SCANDAL MEETS LOVE

Chance of Love

USA TODAY BESTSELLING AUTHOR

Dawn Brower

PROLOGUE

April 1816

Spring had always been her favorite season. Lady Lenora St. Martin didn't have much else to look forward to and the very idea of new beginnings appealed to her. Every spring new life sprouted and the barren landscape was filled with beauty and wonder. That also applied to the London ballrooms. New debutantes were launched in society and the latest crop of true English beauties was put on display for those gentlemen in search of a wife.

Lenora had never been considered a beauty...

She'd accepted her lot in life a long time ago. She had dark brown hair and hazel eyes, both boring. Her attributes along with her shyness kept her position as a wallflower secure. No one noticed her and most of the time that was all right with her. A crowded ballroom tended to bring out her worst anxieties. Her cousin Bennett, the Marquess of Holton, insisted she attend social gatherings. Lenora understood his reasons even if she didn't particularly agree with them. Bennett hoped she'd find a suitor, fall in love, and then marry so she could have a family of her own. All of those things sounded wonderful. None of them were likely to happen. At least not with her...

This ball, the one most debutantes and their mothers clamored to attend, was a good example. The young misses were all flirting with their gentlemen suitors and their mothers gossiped with other matrons. The wallflowers did what they did best—hugged the walls. Lenora; on the other hand, did none of that. She didn't merely stand by the wall hoping some wayward gentleman would discover her and lead her to the dance floor. That would have been too simple and probably preferred by her cousin. No, Lenora didn't do anything by normal standards. She hated to be noticed and would have loved to have remained at home reading one of her favorite novels. So she attempted to make the best of a terrible situation and hid in the darkest most obscure corner she could find.

Spring might mean new beginnings, but it also meant new social gatherings. It led to her greatest discomfort and she dreaded it. If she'd been left alone to walk in the gardens or bask in the warmth of sunlight streaming through her bedroom window she'd have been gloriously happy. Instead she was forced into ballrooms and hiding in corners.

"What's a lovely woman such as yourself doing in this dark corner?" His voice was as warm as honey on a hot summer day. It's tempting sweetness washed over her and made her crave a taste...of something. He was also the biggest rake in all of London. Julian Everleigh, the Duke of Ashley was a notorious seducer. "Come dance with me little mouse."

Lenora wrinkled her nose at his endearment for her. She adored Julian, but she knew better than to accept anything he offered. He visited her cousin often enough she should be unaffected by his flirtations. They thrilled her though and she wanted to savor them whenever he deigned to speak to her. "No thank you," she said softly. "I'm all right, promise."

He chuckled lightly and then tilted his lips

upward into the most sinful smile she'd ever witnessed. Not that she'd seen many... Most gentlemen failed to notice her let alone smile purposely in her direction. "You shouldn't promise something that isn't true little one," he said. "I don't ever bother with a promise because I know myself too well. I'll break them the first chance presented to me." Julian winked at her and it sent flutters through her stomach she'd never felt before in her entire life. "Instead I'll ensure you will never forget dancing with me. I'm quite good at it." He held out his hand. "Now please, do me the honor of spending a few moments with me. I'm in desperate need of protection from unwanted advances." He leaned down just enough so that she could feel his warm breath when he spoke. "Are you willing to be my savior?"

In that moment she'd have promised him anything, but she held back. He said promises were nothing to him. The duke openly admitted to breaking them often. The vow she was about to make would be empty words to him. So instead she smiled, even if it was a little wobbly. Dancing in front of everyone terrified her. "I can try..."

"That's all anyone can ask," he told her.

Why did he have to be so gorgeous? He was too handsome and way too pretty to be paying any attention to her. His golden blond hair rivaled the sun in brilliance and his blue eyes were more dazzling than the most exquisite sapphire. She could easily become lost in his charming veneer if she allowed herself to be. "I supp..suppose," she stuttered over the word. Lenora cleared her throat and began again. "I suppose that is true."

"So?" He lifted a brow. "Will you join me for the next set?"

She nodded as the strands of a waltz filled the room. Lenora almost groaned when she realized what she'd agreed to. The waltz was the most intimate dances and she'd never danced one with a male other than her cousin. Heck, she'd never danced at all with a male besides her cousin... That didn't detract from her dilemma. A waltz with the duke would cause a stir and she'd be so close to him... Her hand shook as she placed it in his. "Lead the way, Your Grace."

He led her to the floor and then he twirled her into the dance before she had time to change her mind, and she'd been close to doing so. The closer she'd stepped toward the light and the prying gazes of the ton she'd become increasingly more anxious. He'd been wise to take the decision away from her.

Julian was an amazing dancer, but that shouldn't have surprised her. Everything about him or that he did seemed to be perfect. "Now," he began. "This doesn't seem so bad does it, little one?"

At least he hadn't called her a mouse again... "No," she agreed. It was actually quite exhilarating. Lenora felt as if she was floating on air.

"I've always considered dancing to be too decadent to be done properly in a public forum," he began. "At least the sort I prefer."

She pushed her eyebrows together. "I'm not sure I follow..."

"I wouldn't expect you would," he replied secretively. "One day you might understand. Perhaps you'll tell me when you do." The corner of his lip turned upward almost...arrogantly. As if only he really understood the secrets of the world...

"I suspect, Your Grace, that our paths won't cross much in the coming years." The duke might be one of her cousin's friends, but she fully expected, at some juncture, to live on her own. Once she reached her majoring in a few months she planned to travel. Maybe to Italy... She hadn't fully decided yet. "We don't keep the same company and in time the little connections we have will dissipate."

"Perhaps," he agreed. "Time will tell I suppose." He twirled her around the floor expertly.

Lenora wouldn't ever forget this moment. She would unlikely never dance again, at least not like this. She was grateful she'd allowed the duke to convince her to participate. Afterward she'd likely find her way to her favorite corner to hide. In her darkest moments she'd be able to travel back to this waltz and recall it, and Julian fondly. If she believed she had a chance of something more with him... She shook that thought away. Loving him was a terrible idea and perhaps the only thing she regretted. This was a kindness, while out of character for him, but she shouldn't expect anything else from him.

The strands of the waltz ended and disappointment filled her. She'd tried to brush his request off at the start and now she never wanted the dance to end. The duke twirled her one last time around the floor and then led her to where their dance had begun. He bowed and kissed her gloved hand. "Thank you for your benevolence, my lady." His blue eyes twinkled with mischief. "And for being my protector when I need it."

She should be thanking him. He had awakened

feelings in her she'd believed long buried. Her heart burst with happiness and affection for this man. "You don't require my protection any more than you needed to dance with me." She frowned. Lenora still couldn't discern his motives for insisting on leading her in the waltz. "Either way the dance was lovely. I'm grateful I didn't insist against it."

He laughed lightly and shook his head. "Little mouse you're always so formal." Julian bowed again. "The pleasure was all mine." He glanced over his shoulder and then back at her. "Pardon me," he said. "I must attend to something important." His smile was bright and appeared genuine. "Enjoy the rest of your evening, my lady." With those words he spun on his heels and headed in the opposite direction.

Lenora smiled as she watched him wander off. She was starting to believe she had misjudged him. He'd been charming, as expected, but also kind and generous with his time. The duke hadn't been required to dance with her. No gentleman was. That made his attention all the more precious to her.

She wandered away from her favorite corner for willingly the first time all evening. Earlier didn't count because Julian had to coax her away from it. Perhaps she should leave the ballroom and explore the gardens. It was starting to become suffocating in the ballroom. Lenora's happiness was nearly bursting from within her. She hugged herself and twirled around as she made her way down the empty hallway leading to the balcony. There was a small staircase on the balcony that led down to the gardens.

Voices echoed back to her. Two male voices to be more precise and both were recognizable.

"Did she dance?" Her cousin asked. Why was Bennett so concerned about her dancing? Why couldn't he leave her to make her own decisions?

"Of course she did," Julian responded. "Do you doubt my ability to charm a woman?" He sounded so...disgusted. Was that because he had to dance with Lenora or because Bennett had doubted his ability? "I can coax any woman to do, well, anything," he boasted. "But a wallflower? That's not even a challenge."

She'd been jubilant until that moment. Now every amount of joy she'd held inside of her deflated in an instant. He'd appeared so kind earlier... How had she gotten it so wrong?

"Attention from you should have caught the notice of all the eligible gentleman in the room," Bennett said. "They'll want to know why the Duke of Ashley bothered with a wallflower. Soon she'll have more callers than she wants."

She didn't want any callers... A part of her hated her cousin for insinuating himself into her life this way. Why did he ask his friend to pay attention to her? Did he hate having her live with him that much? She'd thought they were closer than that...

"I've done you this favor," the duke said. "Don't ask it of me ever again." His tone was harsh and unyielding. It stabbed her in her fragile heart. She'd been on the brink of falling in love with him. The Duke of Ashley didn't deserve her affection. Lenora doubted he was worthy of any woman's love.

Tears stung her eyes and slid down her cheek. She brushed them away with a swipe of her fingertips. They wouldn't help her and they were as useless as her ability to read people. Lenora hardened her heart in that moment. She'd never play the fool again. It was time she learned to weave her way through society without letting another touch her soul again. She'd never be so easily duped again, but she had a lot to learn. There was one person who could teach her and she'd do whatever it took to convince her. That one person was the new Lulia Prescott—the gypsy Duchess of Clare...

With her decision made she rushed out of the

ballroom and walked all the way to the Holton townhouse. She'd need a good night of rest before she started her journey. Her first stop would be Tenby, Wales to visit with the duchess. After that she'd travel as planned. When she returned to London again she'd be an entirely different, better woman.

AFTERWORD

Thank you so much for taking the time to read my book.

Your opinion matters!

Please take a moment to review this book on your favorite review site and share your opinion with fellow readers.

ABOUT THE AUTHOR

USA TODAY Bestselling author, DAWN BROWER writes both historical and contemporary romance. There are always stories inside her head; she just never thought she could make them come to life. That creativity has finally found an outlet.

Growing up she was the only girl out of six children. She is a single mother of two teenage boys; there is never a dull moment in her life. Reading books is her favorite hobby and she loves all genres.

BB bookbub.com/authors/dawn-brower

f facebook.com/AuthorDawnBrower

twitter.com/1DawnBrower

instagram.com/1DawnBrower

Broken Pearl

Deadly Benevolence

A Wallflower's Christmas Kiss

A Gypsy's Christmas Kiss

Snowflake Kisses

Begin Again

There You'll Be

Better as a Memory

Won't Let Go

Enduring Legacy

The Legacy's Origin

Charming Her Rogue

Scandal Meets Love

Love Only Me (Amanda Mariel)

Find Me Love (Dawn Brower)

If It's Love (Amanda Mariel)

Odds of Love (Dawn Brower)

Bluestockings Defying Rogues

When An Earl Turns Wicked

A Lady Hoyden's Secret

One Wicked Kiss

Earl In Trouble

All the Ladies Love Coventry

Marsden Descendants

Rebellious Angel

Tempting An American Princess

Marsden Romances

A Flawed Jewel

A Crystal Angel

A Treasured Lily

A Sanguine Gem

A Hidden Ruby

A Discarded Pearl

Novak Springs

Cowgirl Fever

Dirty Proof

Unbridled Pursuit

Sensual Games

Christmas Temptation

Linked Across Time

Saved by My Blackguard

Searching for My Rogue

Seduction of My Rake

Surrendering to My Spy

Spellbound by My Charmer

Stolen by My Knave

Separated from My Love

Scheming with My Duke

Secluded with My Hellion

Heart's Intent

One Heart to Give

Unveiled Hearts

Heart of the Moment

Kiss My Heart Goodbye

Heart in Waiting

Broken Curses

The Enchanted Princess

The Bespelled Knight

The Magical Hunt

Ever Beloved

Forever My Earl

Always My Viscount

Infinitely My Marquess

Kismet Bay

Once Upon a Christmas

New Year Revelation

All Things Valentine

Luck At First Sight

Coming Soon

Endless Summer Days